MAGGI
CHARLES
The Mirror
Image

Silhouette Special Edition
Published by Silhouette Books New York
America's Publisher of Contemporary Romance

Silhouette Books by Maggi Charles

Magic Crescendo (Rom #134)
Love's Golden Shadow (SE #23)
Love's Tender Trial (SE #45)
The Mirror Image (SE #158)

SILHOUETTE BOOKS, a Division of Simon & Schuster, Inc.
1230 Avenue of the Americas, New York, N.Y. 10020

ISBN: 0-671-53658-3

First Silhouette Books printing April, 1984

10 9 8 7 6 5 4 3 2 1

Map by Ray Lundgren

America's Publisher of Contemporary Romance

Printed in the U.S.A.

BC91

"If You Love Him, You're a Fool to Let Him Go Away Again. . . ."

Without even thinking about, it Tiffany replied, "He never went away from me in the first place."

The words echoed through the little kitchenette. And, for the first time, Tiffany listened to what they were really saying. Alan had never left her, she'd left him. . . .

She shook her head. "It's too late, Trudy."

"I wonder," Trudy answered reflectively.

"Trudy, we've lived without each other for years now. We've gone in two entirely different directions."

"But now," Trudy suggested, "perhaps you've reached a crossroads."

MAGGI CHARLES

is a confirmed traveler who readily admits that "people and places fascinate me." A prolific author, who is also known to her romance fans as Meg Hudson, Ms. Charles states that if she didn't become a writer she would have been a musician having studied the piano and harp. A native New Yorker, she is the mother of two sons and currently resides in Cape Cod, Massachusetts, with her husband.

Dear Reader,

Silhouette Special Editions are an exciting new line of contemporary romances from Silhouette Books. Special Editions are written specifically for our readers who want a story with heightened romantic tension.

Special Editions have all the elements you've enjoyed in Silhouette Romances and *more*. These stories concentrate on romance in a longer, more realistic and sophisticated way, and they feature greater sensual detail.

I hope you enjoy this book and all the wonderful romances from Silhouette.

Karen Solem
Editor-in-Chief
Silhouette Books

To Tiffany Rico . . .
a very special person in
this author's life

The Mirror Image

MASSACHUSETTS,
NEW HAMPSHIRE,
AND MAINE

N
W · E
S

CANADA

MAINE

VERMONT

Bangor

NEW
HAMPSHIRE

Portland

Concord
★

Kennebunk

Portsmouth

ATLANTIC
OCEAN

Cambridge

MASSACHUSETTS

Boston

Cape Cod

CONN.

R.I.

Provincetown

Chapter One

Spring was touching Boston with tentative fingers that early April morning, bringing with it a provocative sense of nostalgia. Tiffany Richards, on her way to work, found herself lingering in the Public Garden, where the trees and shrubs were just beginning to show a hint of green.

This annual renaissance was evoking an unusual restlessness in her. It was Monday, and normally she would have been looking forward to returning to work after the weekend. But this morning she was reluctant to leave Boston's central park.

She crossed the street slowly, then paused at the entrance to the Commonwealth Carlton hotel, thinking wistfully that this would be a great day to play hooky— if one had the right person to play it with.

Once Tiffany entered the hotel's spacious lobby, though, nothing in her poised outward manner gave the slightest hint of this truant inner yearning. Heads turned as she neared the elevator bank, for she was tall, blond and lovely to look at. Today she was wearing a stunning, buff-colored chamois suit, the neutral shade an ideal foil for several pieces from her extensive collection of Navajo turquoise jewelry. She had finished college in New Mexico and had fallen in love with the Indian arts and crafts indigenous to that region of the country.

The bell captain, standing near the elevators, greeted her with a friendly smile. So did one of the assistant managers who happened to pass by just then and two of the front-office employees on their way to work. Tiffany had a special word for each of these people and was also careful to call them by name. People liked to be recognized, she knew, and maintaining a good relationship with the hotel employees was, in her opinion, an important part of her job. As publicity director for Boston's newest luxury hotel, she believed in practicing what her profession preached. In fact, she'd learned to be quite a diplomat. Just the other day the hotel manager had teased that he was afraid one of these days they'd be losing her to the United Nations, she'd become so adept at unraveling snarls that seemed hopelessly tangled.

None of this had come easily, though. Every day Tiffany still voiced a small prayer of thanks to Mike Haggerty, her predecessor in the job and the person from whom she had learned the ropes. A year ago, when Mike lay dying in the coronary care unit at New England Medical Center, he'd found the strength to whisper in her ear, "I've spoken to Grafton Emery about you, Tiffany. And I'm happy to say . . . you can take over. I know you'll be terrific."

Tears had blinded her as she'd stared down at the bluff, middle-aged man whom she'd come to love very much during her two years of working for him. She'd tried to protest, saying, "Mike, look, you'll—" But he'd cut her short.

"It's over for me, Tiffany," he'd told her bravely, "and it's all right."

Thinking about this now as she rode the elevator to the tenth floor, where the hotel's executive offices were located, Tiffany felt tears moisten her eyes. Quickly she daubed them away, for Mike Haggerty had instilled in her one thing she'd never forgotten.

"Always show the world a cheerful face," he'd advised her, his voice betraying a faint Irish brogue even though he'd been born and raised in Boston. "Don't let people get under your skin, especially when you can't see eye to eye with them. If you keep smiling, you'll throw them for a loss. At least most of the time you will. And when the smile doesn't work, you'll know how to take over from there. It's an old cliché, but it's true. You catch more flies with honey than you do with vinegar."

How often during the past twelve months Tiffany had remembered his words, especially at times when it had been difficult to control her temper with those guests who wanted the impossible, or when members of the press insisted upon trying to ferret out stories she couldn't give them. Mike had been right, bless him. Smiling usually paid off. Most of the time things worked out. Crises dissolved; people forgot their differences; the reporters found other stories. And thank God she'd built up a good reputation with the media people. The image of the hotel depended on this.

After stepping out of the elevator at the tenth floor

she turned right and headed toward the publicity offices, midway down the hall. She crossed the threshold of the reception room, ready with a quick, bright good morning for her secretary, Trudy Barnes, who was also a close friend. Then she stopped abruptly, the blithe greeting frozen on her lips.

Trudy was slumped over her desk, her head buried in her arms. Worse, she was moaning!

In an instant Tiffany was at the girl's side, gazing down anxiously at her crumpled, dark red curls. "Trudy, what is it?" she cried urgently.

Trudy raised an agonized face. "I have this awful pain in my side," she managed weakly. "But it'll go away in a minute."

Another look at her secretary convinced Tiffany that this wasn't going to be the case. She grabbed the desk phone and quickly dialed the house nurse's number, remembering that the hotel doctor should be on the premises by now. He usually held a special clinic for employees in the morning, then was available for special consultations until midafternoon.

She heard the nurse's voice and spoke crisply. "Trudy's ill, Betty. She has severe abdominal pain. Can Dr. Heatherton come up and take a look at her?"

Trudy was trying to sit upright, protesting that she was fine, but it was a dismal, though valiant, attempt. Soon after the doctor arrived she was ready to accept the fact that she was headed for the hospital—and an emergency appendectomy.

By this time Grafton Emery, the hotel manager, had hurried in from his suite just down the hall, and several other executives and their secretaries were on the scene as well. After Trudy had been whisked away in an ambulance, Tiffany gently but firmly cleared her premises of all the curious onlookers. Only Grafton Emery lingered.

He was a tall, distinguished man, prematurely gray. Actually, his hair was silvery, and he tended to wear light gray suits that played up its effect. Attractive? Yes, Tiffany conceded, there was no doubt at all that Grafton was very attractive. He was also a widower, and of late he'd been making it fairly obvious to Tiffany that he might be considered available.

Thus far she'd not gone out with him alone. But they frequently lunched or dined together in the hotel with others on the executive staff, Grafton usually managing to arrange the seating so that she wound up at his side. His attention was flattering, of course. Grafton Emery was an urbane, sophisticated man of the world, probably twenty years her senior, Tiffany surmised. She was just shy of twenty-nine, and Grafton, she estimated, must be in his late forties. Still, he was a vigorous man who took very good care of himself.

Recently Tiffany and Grafton had been discussing the possibility of playing some tennis together now that spring was just over the horizon. Grafton belonged to an exclusive tennis club, and he'd already told her that he'd like her to be his guest there. She was looking forward to this, although she was wary of becoming too involved with him. If she were looking for involvement, she conceded privately, it was true that Grafton would be an excellent candidate. She didn't doubt that he'd be an accomplished, considerate lover. And she almost wished she could consider having an affair with him. It would be wonderful to have someone to whom she could respond with enthusiasm in this area of her life. But she had been burned, severely hurt, and in the eight years since her marriage had broken up she'd found it impossible to make any real commitment to a man. Thus, although she was a thoroughly human young woman she'd remained . . . well, the word would be *celibate,* Tiffany decided, and smiled wryly at the thought.

Grafton, seated in one of the office's two comfortable lounge chairs, caught her smile. "Care to share the joke?" he suggested.

"I would . . . if there were one," Tiffany told him, assuming her place behind the large, pale birch desk that was the focal point of the room. Sitting at the desk gave her a sense of security. There was a comforting expanse of wood in front of her serving as a definite barrier. Grafton, she thought—and again had to suppress her amusement—was far too much of a gentleman to storm such a citadel without definite encouragement.

Her thoughts returned to the incident that had just taken place. "Poor Trudy," she sighed, remembering her secretary's stricken face. "She was in such pain."

"A week from now she'll be better than new," Grafton commented blandly. "But in the meantime this leaves you shorthanded. I'll see if sales can spare you a girl, unless you'd prefer to call one of the temporary secretarial help services."

"If Rob has someone he can lend me, I'd rather go that route," Tiffany said, referring to Robert LeBaron, who was the hotel's sales manager. and thus empowered with the task of booking conventions and other large groups. "Any girl who works in sales will have an idea of what goes on here, whereas someone from the outside . . ."

"I'll speak to him this morning," Grafton promised, and Tiffany had no doubt that a substitute secretary would be available to her before the end of the day. "Two of my girls are on vacation this week," he went on, "otherwise I'd let you borrow one of them. As it is . . ." He shrugged, then rose slowly. "I'd better be getting back," he said resignedly. "Mondays. I always find them hard to cope with, especially at this time of year. It wouldn't take much to convince me to ditch the whole thing and escape with you for some tennis."

"Stop daydreaming, Grafton," Tiffany teased lightly. "You're only making it tougher to face reality!"

This was true. After the manager had left her office, she emerged from behind her desk and walked over to the big picture window that overlooked the Public Garden and the Common. A day like today brought back memories, many of them bittersweet. Tiffany found herself thinking of her childhood days in the big family house in Upstate New York, where towering willow trees fringed the pond at the back of the property. They were always the first to give a sign of spring, turning gold-green even before the crocuses popped up through the warm earth. Alan had asked her to marry him one summer Sunday afternoon as they'd walked along the side of that pond, the grass stubbly beneath their feet. "Yes! Oh, yes!" she'd answered promptly, and had fallen into his arms, suffused with her love for him . . . a young, vulnerable love.

Tiffany forced herself away from both the window and her thoughts. The past was the past, the present was the present, she reminded herself. If she'd learned anything at all, she'd learned that basic tenet. Also, there was plenty of work to be done.

First there was a message from *The Boston Globe* insisting that an important movie star was staying in the hotel incognito . . . which, as it happened, was true.

The dilemma was how to protect the client's privacy and at the same time manage to maintain good relations with the press. Then the housekeeper called to report that a valuable gold and diamond watch had been found by one of the maids. The question here was whether or not to notify the man who'd occupied the room over the weekend, because there was always a chance that the lady registered with him had not been his wife!

Also, Tiffany had requested VIP accommodations for a well-known television commentator who was arriving from New York to do a special broadcast in Boston. But when midmorning rolled around, the front office manager himself burst into her office, clearly disturbed.

Fred Bates was a gangling, skinny man with an engaging personality, usually the life of any staff party. Right now, though, he was frenzied. "We have that medical group arriving this morning for five days of meetings," he pointed out. "Important meetings! You got their advance publicity, I imagine."

Tiffany nodded calmly. "I was planning on tackling that later this afternoon," she said. "It was the first thing on my agenda, but with Trudy out . . ."

"Of course," Fred Bates agreed. "I'd say some good stories should come out of their sessions, though."

"I'm sure they will."

"Okay, Tiffany. The thing of it is, the doctors are filling up the best rooms in the house. A number of them wanted suites so they could entertain or hold separate conferences with their colleagues. Anyway, I don't have anything choice left over for your man from the network. In fact, we're just about BTC."

Tiffany knew that even when the hotel was allegedly

"booked to capacity," there were usually a few empty rooms held for any latecoming VIPs.

"Fred," she said patiently, "Hank Carella asked me to make this reservation . . . and, as you know, he *is* Mr. Boston TV. Vernon Platt is a personal friend of his, and he's internationally famous. I really want him to have a suite."

"Tiffany . . ."

She smiled sweetly. "Hank promised me that if we do well for Mr. Platt he'll be sure to mention where his friend is staying while he's in town. Prime time, Fred. Boston's hottest show. A credit like that would give us a lot more mileage than any of your doctors might, right?"

"Touché," the front office manager answered unhappily. "Okay . . . I'll see if I can do some juggling."

After Fred Bates's departure the morning continued on an even busier course, and when noon came Tiffany knew that some of the routine details had, of necessity, been skipped. One task that Trudy took care of first thing every day was to go over the duplicate list of guest registrations, this furnished to the publicity office by the front office at nine o'clock each morning. Prominent names were noted, and unless those guests had specifically requested privacy, their names were released to the various news sources. This type of cooperation was one sure way of having the hotel favorably mentioned, Tiffany had learned.

This morning there simply had not been time to go over the "dupes," nor was she in the mood to attend to the task before lunch. She promised herself she'd get to the registrations early in the afternoon—provided nothing else happened to alter her schedule—and would also thoroughly scan the medical group's advance releases. There might very well be some excellent stories in the making, as Fred Bates had suggested.

Just now, though, she needed a break from the pace of the morning. And when Robert LeBaron stopped by to ask if she'd be joining the other members of the executive staff for lunch in the Veranda Room, it was easy to say, "Not today, Rob. But thanks anyway."

"Sally Grant will be in to help you just as soon as she finishes up a couple of things for me," Rob LeBaron said then. "She's good, Tiffany. Efficient, quick, responsible. You can have her until Trudy gets back."

Tiffany grinned. "That's pretty noble of you, Rob," she told the pleasant, balding sales manager. "I really appreciate it."

"Well, maybe you can get them to put me on the cover of *Time* as Man of the Year!" Rob quipped.

"I'll look into it," Tiffany said, laughing.

After Rob LeBaron left, it suddenly occurred to her that promoting a story on the sales manager might not be such a bad idea. There was a lot to handling conventions, group functions and special events in a large hotel such as the Commonwealth Carlton. Rob's job was fascinating, and he performed it very well. Anyway, he deserved a little publicity.

She paused next to call the hospital. Trudy was still in surgery, so there was no real word to be had about her condition.

Hanging up the phone receiver, Tiffany sighed deeply. Although she'd been trying to function efficiently all morning, worry about Trudy had been distracting her. Over the months they'd achieved a close personal relationship. They were both divorced, so this had been an initial common bond. But their friendship had developed way beyond that. Trudy had become almost like the sister Tiffany'd never had.

She glanced around her office to make sure that everything was in relatively good order, then started out. As she left the hotel she forced her thoughts away from Trudy and reminded herself again to try to plant a story about Rob LeBaron. Sometimes it was easy to forget the good story material right under one's eyes.

She was expanding on this concept as she walked over to Newbury Street, pausing at a salad bar for a special concoction on Syrian bread. There were a lot of good potential stories right "in house" at the hotel.

Lunch finished, Tiffany window-shopped on her way back to the hotel, her footsteps admittedly lagging. Golden sunlight filtered down onto the city streets, its warmth like a caress after winter. Again she was aware of spring's stirring—and of her own unusually deep response to it.

Reluctantly she continued on. She knew that the work load was going to be heavy this afternoon, and Sally Grant, unfamiliar with the workings of the publicity office, would need help. Tiffany would have to be on hand to advise Sally, and she also had a number of things to attend to herself. A problem with public relations was that time was always a limiting factor. Breaking news stories, for instance, wouldn't wait.

What to approach first? As she entered the elevator, her gaze momentarily downcast, Tiffany was wondering whether she could trust Sally to handle the duplicates on her own. Would Sally be familiar enough with "names" to recognize their potential for generating news? Would she realize the importance of certain other guests, guests who might not be newsworthy, but who nevertheless would warrant special attention? It was always nice to send flowers to their rooms, or perhaps a basket of fruit, or even a bottle of champagne.

Thinking this, Tiffany concluded that she'd better do the dupes herself, and reached out to press the button for the tenth floor . . . only to encounter a long, masculine finger involved in doing exactly the same thing. Catching her breath, she froze. You couldn't identify someone by touching a single finger. You couldn't! Yet this instant of contact was so electric, so searing, that for an agonized second Tiffany was actually afraid to look up at the man who was sharing the elevator with her.

She was conscious of the metal doors sliding shut; she heard the faint whir of machinery and felt the upward thrust of the boxlike structure. Then, slowly, she looked up. Her eyes were deep, dark pools, and she had no idea how eloquent they were as she raised them to meet a searingly familiar steel-gray gaze.

His name stuck in her throat. She could not possibly have spoken it aloud. She saw his lips tighten, a telltale muscle twitch in his jaw. Then something seemed to flicker in those clear eyes, tiny, needle-sharp shards of light.

"Tiffany!" he said hoarsely.

She felt as if her breath were being sucked into a vacuum, as if she had climbed a long flight of stairs too fast. She wanted to escape . . . and stared frantically at the elevator's blank walls as if suddenly a magic ladder might dangle before her, a way out.

Oh, my God! she moaned silently to herself. Deep inside her, each word echoed with a muted agony too intense to verbalize. Oh, my God . . . *Alan!*

*   *   *

Alan Winslow was accustomed to controlling his emotions. He was a surgeon, and an air of confidence, of objectivity, was essential to his work. But as he stared down at Tiffany he knew that his mask had been stripped away and placed on the highest possible shelf, far beyond his reach.

She was so beautiful. Far more beautiful in early maturity than she'd been as a young girl. This conclusion came unbidden as he scanned her face, noting the eyes, which were as dark and mysterious as they'd always been, and the shimmering, pale blond hair that she no longer wore flowing freely around her shoulders. It was pulled back now into something very simple, something very elegant. He clung to this word. Elegant.

Tiffany was tall—she came slightly above Alan's shoulder when she had shoes with heels on, as she did now, and he was well over six feet. She was also very slim—quite a bit thinner than she'd been the last time he'd seen her—yet her figure still was curved in all the right places. Alan didn't know much about women's clothes, or at least he'd never paid much attention to them, but at once he noticed how tasteful and appealing Tiffany's were. Her outfit was perfectly coordinated, even to the tan and brown plaid blouse, with its neat little collar. It looked understated yet provocatively feminine. It also emphasized what seemed, to Alan, a new sophistication about her. Yet her perfume, at least, was the same. Its enticing fragrance, a blend of flowers and spice, assailed his nostrils, and memories he didn't think he could cope with came sweeping over him in waves. This was surf too rough to ride, and swallowing hard, he knew he'd mumbled her name aloud, his voice darkly abrasive.

It had been eight years since he'd last seen her, since she'd walked out of his life to put the better part of a continent between them. He'd been overwhelmingly hurt at first. Then, when logic had finally taken over and he'd known he should go after her and follow her to the ends of the earth if necessary, he'd had neither the time nor the spirit to do so. He'd been starting his second year of surgical residency at Albany Medical Center, and too much had happened.

He'd been stupid enough, proud enough, in the beginning to think Tiffany would come back. And he still remembered the shock of the divorce papers that had arrived one day from a firm in Albuquerque. Albuquerque, New Mexico. Distraught, he'd wondered what in God's name Tiffany had been doing out there. He'd tried to contact her through her attorney, but she had refused to communicate with him.

It had been too much, the last straw that broke the camel's back, and Alan had crumbled. He hadn't cared about the grounds on which she was suing him, he'd patently ignored the details, nor had contesting the divorce ever occurred to him. She'd made it clear that they'd come to the end of their road, and, God knows, she'd had reason enough to believe that. Now, eight years later, he could look back and realize so many things he hadn't understood then.

Did the same thing apply to her? he wondered. Did Tiffany ever look back, or try to second-guess her actions? What was she thinking? She was white as a sheet, her pupils dilated, her breath coming fast. But he couldn't credit himself with any plusses for this reaction. Obviously there was no pleasure for her in seeing him again.

For a long moment they both seemed suspended in

space, together in the tiny enclosed box moving slowly upward, yet too fast at that. They reached the tenth floor; the elevator shuddered slightly as it came to a stop. Then the doors slid open, and it was only natural that he wait for her to precede him, after which he stepped out into a hall carpeted in tones of blue, green and turquoise, this last shade, he noticed, identical to that of the jewelry she was wearing.

Her face was tense, very tense. So tense that it caused him a brief flash of professional worry. "Tiffany . . ." he managed.

"Alan."

She spoke his name flatly.

"Please," he said. "I've got to talk to you." The words, bouncing against his eardrums, sounded so terribly trite.

"No," she said immediately, then added, less emphatically, "we've nothing to talk about."

"Must we be enemies, Tiffany?" The question startled him, seeming to spring straight from his subconscious, and he saw Tiffany's eyes widen, as if he'd shocked her.

"I don't consider you an enemy, Alan," she said slowly.

"Thank you," he returned simply.

For a moment she stared at him, and he suspected she was close to tears. Then, almost imploringly, she said, "Please . . . I must go."

Alan hesitated, desperately anxious to make his next move the right one. He wanted to take her aside someplace where they could be alone, someplace where they could sit down and talk. Because regardless of what she'd said, in his opinion they had a great deal to talk about.

But while he stood, irresolute, the moment—the chance—became lost to him. "If you'll excuse me," Tiffany said, and now her pallor really alarmed him. He had to fight the impulse to reach out, grasp her wrist and search for a pulse. He saw that she really *was* shocked, terribly shocked, and was appalled to realize how much he'd shaken her.

"Please," she said again, and he saw he was blocking her way. He stepped aside instinctively, and she brushed past him, turning to the right. His room was to the left, and after a long, tortured moment, he turned and walked away from her.

Tiffany wanted to look back. She desperately wanted to look back. She had to force herself to continue down the hall, and it was a relief to see Sally Grant sitting at Trudy's desk.

Sally was a plump, cheerful girl. "Phone messages galore," she said by way of greeting, and held out a sheath of notes. "I thought I'd better take them all down and let you decide which ones you'd like me to handle."

Tiffany nodded weakly, still in shock. She clutched the notes Sally passed her, and their hands touched. Surprised, Sally said, "Your fingers are freezing."

"Cold hands, warm heart," Tiffany quipped, and tried to manage a smile. Fortunately Sally didn't know her well enough to recognize what a dismal facsimile of the real thing this particular smile was. "I'll go over these right away," she added, taking a deep breath. "Anything urgent, do you know?"

"The *Globe* food columnist phoned," Sally answered. "He wanted to be sure that two o'clock was still okay for his interview with René Gervais. I checked your appointment pad and you had it down, so I told him it was."

Tiffany had completely forgotten that the *Globe* was going to do a feature story on the Commonwealth Carlton's proud new acquisition, a chef straight from a five star restaurant in Paris. "I'll have to sit in on that," she said absently.

In her office she quickly scanned the phone messages Sally had taken, marking answers on the ones Sally could handle and putting aside the rest of them to be dealt with as her time allowed. Then she glanced at her appointment pad to make certain she wasn't suffering any more memory lapses and discovered that she'd also forgotten about the special staff meeting Grafton Emery had called for four o'clock. This would undoubtedly stretch into the cocktail hour. Tiffany sighed. At the moment she hardly felt like participating in what would amount to a lot of social chitchat.

On the other hand, she conceded, almost anything would be better than being alone. Alan had been the last person in the world she'd expected to see today, and the encounter had rocked her badly.

He was even better looking than he'd been when he was younger, she decided. But there was a new aloofness in his manner, an assurance. Despite his own shock at seeing her—and that had been obvious—he had given her the impression of a person totally in command of himself. That shouldn't be so surprising though, she reminded herself. He'd been on the road to command for a long, long time.

Also, something new had been added. Something that hurt in a way she couldn't explain. There were touches of silver at his temples, certainly becoming,

and not exactly premature. Alan was thirty-five, after
all. Still, Tiffany felt a pang of emotion thinking of
them. She had always loved his deep chestnut hair, so
soft to the touch. She had loved to run her fingers
through its velvet smoothness. So often this tenderness,
this pleasure, had been the prelude to their wonderful
lovemaking. . . .

She shut off her thoughts impatiently and picked up
the telephone, to dial the hospital again. Trudy was out
of surgery and in the recovery room. There was
nothing more to be learned at the moment, so Tiffany
turned her attention to the most important message. A
minute later she was talking to the fashion director at a
large department store about putting on a fashion show
on the hotel's new roof garden, which would open
officially on the first of May.

One call followed another, and then it was time to
visit the hotel's extensive kitchens with the *Globe*
writer while he interviewed the chef, this in itself
something of a Gallic explosion, for René Gervais was
temperamental, to say the least. After that she sat in on
the staff conference but managed to leave before
Grafton could suggest that they all go down to the
lounge for a drink.

Only then, back in her office with Sally gone for the
day, did she have time to approach the neglected
duplicate registrations. These, she knew, would reveal
what room Alan Winslow was staying in . . . and why
he was here at all.

Chapter Two

$\mathcal{D}$r. Alan Winslow, Eastern Maine Medical Center, Bangor, Maine. The name leapt out boldly from the other registrations, and Tiffany found herself staring at it as if she were hypnotized.

Maine. She'd assumed Alan had stayed on at Albany Medical Center after finishing his surgical residency there. She tabulated briefly. He'd been a second year resident with three years to go when she'd left him. After that, chances were he had trained further as a specialist. Two more years, perhaps three, would have passed. Certainly, he had been a full-fledged surgeon for . . . how long now? At least two years, she estimated. Possibly longer.

At what point had he left Albany to move to Maine? Strange how one's concepts could be altered so swiftly. Whenever she'd thought of him—as she had much too often, especially in the beginning—she'd also conjured up images of New York State's capital, the city where she'd been born and brought up.

Many times she'd met Alan at the hospital, but she'd never gone inside. She'd been painfully conscious of the fact that this was his world, not hers, a large part of his life in which she really had no place, even though she was tremendously proud of him. She'd always met him in the parking lot, and now she remembered Alan, dressed in jeans and a bulky Aran sweater, waiting for her on a crisp autumn afternoon. Alan, unshaven and exhausted, shadows beneath his eyes after a long, rough weekend on call with only five or six hours of sleep.

The Alan she'd met in the elevator this afternoon had come a long way from that tired, sometimes disheveled young resident. This "new" Alan was disturbingly attractive—not that Alan hadn't always been both disturbing and attractive to her. But there was something different about the man she'd encountered this afternoon. Maturity . . . yes, that was part of it. But she'd also sensed a latent strength in him; it was as if his character had been shaped anew, forged out of . . . suffering.

The word threw her. Because she'd never, until this moment, accepted the fact that Alan had suffered too. . . .

Tiffany drew a long, ragged breath. Then, summoning self-discipline, she forced herself to get back to business. Quickly she scanned through the rest of the registrations, noting that there were several celebrities in the house who might make interesting copy. A well-known makeup artist from Hollywood was visiting Boston, and an impressionist who'd caused quite a stir in New York was in town for a week-long, one-man show. Tiffany made phone calls to the right sources and agreed to set up interviews if the people in question were receptive to the idea of a little publicity—as they almost surely would be.

Next she turned her attention to answering the rest of the phone messages Sally Grant had taken down for her. Two calls were personal in nature, and she found herself declining a dinner invitation for that night and hedging on a luncheon date for tomorrow. Finally she'd finished the last of the details—with one exception. The medical group would be meeting all week, and after glancing at only a few of the names in attendance, Tiffany fully realized what excellent material would be generated from many of their sessions.

Alan was among the group, she had no doubt of that. She referred back to the dupes to verify his arrival and departure dates and was chagrined to find that he was booked into his suite for three extra days, which meant he would be a guest at the Commonwealth Carlton through the following Monday. She frowned. The thought of working for an entire week with Alan on the premises was disconcerting, at the very least. Also, she wondered why he was staying so long. The group had scheduled its banquet for Friday night, and surely most of the doctors would be checking out Saturday morning.

Did Alan have business that would be keeping him in Boston? Business . . . or pleasure?

Tiffany looked more closely at the list and discovered that many of the male doctors had brought their wives along with them for the week. This, though, was hardly unusual. There was always plenty for the women to do, whether or not they attended the meetings. That thought prompted yet another idea for a story. Perhaps a feature about medical wives could be planted somewhere. Doctors were supposed to have the highest divorce rate in the country, next to policemen, Tiffany had heard.

She smiled wryly. She'd certainly done her bit in keeping up those statistics!

"Working late, Tiffany?" a voice inquired, jolting her. Grafton Emery was standing in the doorway.

"Just tying up a few odds and ends," she said, striving for a casual tone. She didn't want to arouse any suspicions in Grafton. The less he knew about Alan Winslow, the better.

"Any word on Trudy?"

"She was in the recovery room last time I called," Tiffany reported. "I was just about to try again to see if I can find out something more."

"Mind if I wait around?" Grafton asked.

Tiffany, already searching in the phone book again for the hospital's number, shook her head. But she was very much aware of Grafton's eyes upon her as she placed the call through the hotel switchboard, then asked for patient information and was told that Miss Barnes was out of the recovery room and doing well.

"I'll get over to see her tomorrow at lunchtime," she decided, hanging up the phone and breathing a small sigh of relief.

"Remind me to send flowers," Grafton said.

"I will."

"Tiffany . . ."

"Yes?"

"You seemed a bit . . . distracted at the staff meeting this afternoon. Nothing wrong, is there?"

Grafton Emery was astute, and also inquisitive. The combination could be trying at times.

"No," she answered almost too hastily. "I was preoccupied, that's all." She flashed a smile at him. "And I'd just come up from that interview the *Globe* food columnist had with René Gervais. It seems that Monsieur Gervais is not the easiest man in the world to ask questions of. He's . . . well, he's rather temperamental, shall we say?"

"So I've heard."

"Anyway, they didn't exactly see eye to eye about things like nouvelle cuisine!"

Grafton chuckled. "Who won?" he asked.

"Our chef," Tiffany said, and had to laugh herself, adding, "despite the fact that his command of the English language is close to nonexistent, Monsieur Gervais definitely managed to hold his own."

The hotel manager rose. He was a lithe, attractive man, his vivid blue tie bringing out the deep color of his eyes. For a moment those eyes held hers. Then, to Tiffany's relief, he wrested his gaze away and moved, with obvious reluctance, toward the door.

"Get some rest," he suggested in parting. "You look tired."

Tiffany was tired. Very tired. But she was also restless. Normally Monday night would have been one of the three evenings a week she went to a dance studio in the Back Bay to lose herself to the intricate strains of jazz. There was a freedom to modern dance, jazz ballet—whatever one called it; she loved it and was quite good. Dancing helped keep her in shape—tennis, her favorite sport, wasn't always convenient in the city—and also unlocked all sorts of tensions. For her it was an emotional release as well as satisfying physical exercise.

Probably she needed this outlet tonight more than she usually did. Yet she found herself bypassing the studio and heading for her apartment in the Bay Towers, an attractive complex overlooking Boston Harbor. Through a glorious April twilight she walked along the length of Charles Street, then hailed a taxi to take her the rest of the way home.

Tiffany's apartment was clearly a reflection of her personality. She'd tastefully blended the modern and the antique, and had highlighted mostly subdued tones with unexpected splashes of deep color. The walls in her living room were white, her long couch a vivid burnt orange, and both here and in her bedroom the art was entirely Spanish-American, collected lovingly during her years in New Mexico.

Her furniture was designed in the Spanish mission style, and her china was Mexican, as were the several prominently displayed pieces of silver she cherished. She'd bought those particular items in the town of Taxco de Alarcón, fifty miles southwest of Mexico City. The wall in the dinette area was dominated by a huge clay plate enameled in a rich pattern of tropical colors set against a black base. This she had bought in Oaxaca, from the woman who had made it.

She'd tried very hard to create a new life for herself. She'd tried to wash away the memories of her marriage. She'd brought nothing that might remind her of Alan to Boston—not even a single photograph. But she'd not been able to blot out the pictures of him that lingered persistently in her mind.

She had loved him so much, so very much. He'd been her first love. She amended that. Her only love.

Thinking about this, Tiffany poured herself a glass of chilled Chablis and turned on the stereo. Mellow guitar strumming filled the room. Early Beatles, Paul McCartney singing "Yesterday." The song brought back all sorts of memories, but this was something she had learned to live with. She couldn't shut out beautiful music, even though certain songs could be too evocative of the past; they could stir her emotions more profoundly than almost anything else.

First love. She sat down on the couch, twirling the stem of her wineglass between long, slim fingers. The phrase always sounded a bit frothy. Pink frills, wrist corsages, the senior prom, heavy petting in the back seat of a borrowed car. These associations automatically came to mind, yet her first love had been nothing like that, nothing at all like that.

She'd been nineteen, had just finished her first year of college and knew she wanted to go into public relations. In fact, she had a summer job with a local agency as a girl Friday, which she soon learned meant fetching and carrying for the copywriters and making sure there was always an adequate supply of fresh hot coffee at hand.

Alan had recently been graduated from medical school and had one month's vacation before starting on his surgical residency at Albany Medical Center. They had both been invited to a "beginning of summer party" mutual friends were giving at their place on a bluff overlooking Lake George. It was early in the season, so the resort wasn't yet too crowded.

Tiffany had owned a Volkswagen in those days, a bright yellow Bug that she loved and was very proud of. Unfortunately the little car had weathered a lot of travel before she'd acquired it. Finally it had begun to give her trouble. She'd been about a mile down the turnoff road to the Baldwins' home when the car had started belching smoke, then suddenly sputtered to a halt.

Alan had driven up behind her at that point and, witnessing her struggles, had pulled his own rather ancient MG over to the side of the road. He'd diagnosed the Volkswagen's trouble much too quickly—besides burning oil, the carburetor was filthy, he'd said. Although he had been quite decent about imparting this information to her, Tiffany had sensed his amusement and had been thoroughly chagrined.

"Too bad," he'd observed laconically. "The engine sort of suffocated, you might say."

She'd glanced up at him swiftly. She'd been used to meeting men on an eye to eye level, for the simple reason that she'd been five feet ten inches tall since she was thirteen years old. Her height was something she'd come to accept. But she'd had to tilt her head back to look at him, and for the first time she'd met that disturbing gray glance she would never forget.

His eyes were so clear. A pure, true gray. She was to find that they could be icy cold or as searing as hot metal, but on that first encounter she only knew that he was taking in all of her, just as she was staring at him. And when he flashed her a heart-stopping smile, she could only conclude that he liked what he saw.

"Hop in," he'd invited then, gesturing toward his car. "I'll take you to the nearest gas station. There's one just down the road."

"I think we're closer to the place where I'm going," Tiffany had countered. "Maybe I can get some help there."

"Where were you heading?"

"The place is called Blue Pines," Tiffany had told him. "It belongs to friends of mine."

"The Baldwins?"

"Yes."

"I'm going there too," he'd replied with considerable satisfaction.

So they'd arrived at the Baldwins' house together, had returned to retrieve her car, and had become inseparable for the rest of the weekend. The water had been too cold for swimming, but the Baldwins owned their own tennis court, and Alan shared Tiffany's enthusiasm for the game. Except that he was more adept at it than she was, she'd learned, once they'd played a couple of sets.

Later, as they were strolling back to the house, he'd said, "For the past eight years I haven't had much time for tennis . . . or for anything else really relaxing."

"The past eight years?" she'd queried.

"College, then med school," he'd informed her.

She'd stared at him. "You're a doctor?"

"Just, actually. I graduated two weeks ago."

"I don't believe it. You look so . . . young."

He'd laughed. "I'll be twenty-six in November."

"Still . . ."

"Don't worry," he'd said lightly. "They'll keep watch over me while I'm wielding a scalpel!"

"You're a surgeon?"

"I hope to be a surgeon," he'd corrected. Then he'd told her about the residency coming up at Albany Medical Center, and Tiffany tried not to be too obvious about the exultant feeling this gave her. He'd be in Albany for five years. Five years! Skidmore College, where she was going to school, was in Saratoga Springs, less than an hour away.

That Sunday afternoon they'd gone sailing on the lake. Tiffany had worn a hooded wool pullover, but there was a chill to the wind that made her cheeks feel as if they were being frosted. Alan, who'd handled the boat masterfully, had been disturbingly attractive in a loose gray sweat shirt and faded blue jeans rolled up to his knees. Tiffany had been deeply stirred by the impact of his masculinity and was painfully conscious of his proximity. The wind ruffled his deep brown hair, and they'd been out of doors so much during the weekend that his skin had acquired a ruddy tone. In her opinion he was everything a man should be, and she felt a surge of purely primitive desire that rocked her body with its potency.

Tiffany was an only child. Her father was a lawyer, her mother a concert organist. They were sophisticated people, yet they'd brought their daughter up to believe in a moral code that was stricter than the one being followed by most of her contemporaries. Because of this she was still a virgin.

She'd always been popular. The lovely old frame house in which she lived, shaded by gracious elms and oaks, was always open to her friends, and both the boys and girls she knew had loved to come there. Tiffany had gone through a few high school crushes, had spurned a college classmate who wanted much more than she was willing to give him, and had been stirred, occasionally, by a kiss, especially if there was moonlight for a backdrop and soft music playing nearby. Never before, though, had she come to grips with anything like this wild, pulsating craving she was feeling for Alan Winslow.

At that moment he'd looked down at her. Their

gazes held fast, and the message was clear. It was mutual. She wanted him, he wanted her. *Want?* My God, this was much more than "wanting." This was a cascading form of torture, making her writhe in anticipated ecstasy.

She had no idea what might have happened next if the boat had not capsized—what he might have said to her, what course of action they might have followed. As it was, they'd been sailing along smoothly one minute, then had suddenly heeled sharply. Angry gusts streaked across the lake from nowhere, and even as Alan was shouting a warning to her they went over. Tiffany'd felt the lake's cold water permeate her clothing and knew a moment of panic. Instinctively she started to tread, but then Alan's arms closed around her.

"Can you swim?" he'd asked anxiously.

She'd nodded numbly.

"Okay," he'd said. "Now listen. We've got to get the boat righted. At least I'd like to . . . before someone on shore sees us and comes blasting out here to the rescue."

This, though, was exactly what had happened. What seemed to Tiffany like a convoy of powerboats had converged on them, and then she was being lifted aboard one of them . . . and separated from Alan entirely.

Much later, when the other houseguests were all watching an old movie on TV, he'd whispered in her ear, "Come take a walk, will you?"

Tiffany had quietly followed him out the back door, then down the path that led to the lake. The moon had been three-quarters full that night and had cast a shimmering band of silver across the dark water. Alan had groped for her hand; she'd felt his fingers, warm and sure. "My God, I was terrified," he'd said.

"You?" she'd asked, surprised. "I wouldn't have thought anything could have terrified you."

"The idea of you drowning did," he'd answered grimly. "I didn't have the sense to ask you if you could swim before I took you out. I just assumed . . ."

"I've been swimming all my life," Tiffany had blurted, exaggerating only slightly.

"It's a damned good thing. If you'd panicked . . ."

She'd come reasonably close to panicking, but she wasn't about to tell him so. Anyway, there hadn't been time to utter a word, for at that moment Alan had turned her toward him, and in another instant she was in his arms. Their lips met, the kiss deepening as his tongue began to probe her mouth, gently, tenderly at first, little explorations that set the warm, treacherous stream she'd felt earlier flowing through her once again. Then the intensity of his kisses increased as his hands began to fervently caress her, sliding beneath her sweater.

"Oh, my God," he'd groaned. "You're so beautiful, Tiffany . . . and I'm so insane about you!"

After that he'd drawn her closer and, with a shock of pleasure, Tiffany had felt his maleness and realized how fully aroused he'd become. They'd stood wrapped in each others arms, possessed by a mutual urgency and feeling helplessly frustrated because this was neither the time nor the place in which they could express their love. There were too many other people around, there was no privacy. So, reluctantly, they'd turned back toward the house.

The next weekend Alan had called to tell her that he was in Albany. She'd invited him for Sunday dinner, and afterward they'd gone for a walk along the shore of the willow-fringed pond. Out of sight of the house, he'd pulled her into his arms and kissed her deeply and passionately. Any possible defenses Tiffany might have been able to summon had blown away like a house of cards ruffled by the wind. Inexperienced though she'd been, she'd known he could have easily taken her right then under the drooping branches. And she'd realized that he knew this, too.

Instead, Alan had stepped back to look down at her gravely. "I've always sworn I wouldn't get married until I was established," he'd said, his voice deep, "but at least I'm through med school, and I'm on the way." He'd looked far into her eyes then and had added huskily, "I don't think I can go on living without you, Tiffany."

She'd been certain she couldn't go on living without him. So, despite her parents' protests that this was all happening much too quickly, she and Alan were married later that month, a week before he began his internship in Albany.

Spring's twilight had faded. It was dark in the room, and her wineglass had been empty for a long time. The stereo cassette had finished playing too. Tiffany switched on a light, then stood slowly, her mood reflective.

Resolutely she went out to the kitchen, picked up the bottle of Chablis, and poured herself another glass. The wine had a refreshing tang, and she forced herself to savor and appreciate its qualities. Confront the moment—and take the best from it. Experience had taught her this was one way to get through things, to get over traumas.

Philosopher! Tiffany had also learned to laugh at herself, and she did so now, though it was shaky laughter nonetheless. Then she searched the contents of her refrigerator, knowing that although she was not at all hungry she really needed to eat something.

Briefly she wished she'd accepted Hank Carella's invitation to go out to dinner . . . or better still, that she had invited him over for a home-cooked Chinese meal. These past couple of years she'd been getting more proficient at Oriental cooking and really enjoyed both preparing the food—time consuming though that could be—and devouring the succulent results. She'd become skillful at stir-frying—her Wok was one of her favorite kitchen utensils—and she prided herself on the perfectly steamed rice that accompanied most of the dishes she served.

She could have used Hank's easy brand of companionship tonight . . . and the thought occurred that she might even have let him make love to her. Like herself, he'd been burned. He'd gone through a traumatic divorce and thus far had shied away from marrying again as much as she had. He had a terrific career as one of Boston's leading TV personalities and also did a scintillating, thrice-weekly "local scenes" column for the *Globe*. Hank knew all the right people, could get front row tickets to any performance, commanded the best tables in the best restaurants and managed all of this with an understated approach that was . . . well, whimsical was what it was, Tiffany decided.

Hank was tall and dark and too thin. He ate like the

proverbial horse, and she believed what he'd told her when they'd first met—he could eat his own weight daily and never gain an ounce. He had thinning black hair, a rugged, almost homely face and the most engaging smile she'd ever seen.

She corrected that. Almost the most engaging smile she'd ever seen. Alan . . .

She slammed on the mental brakes again. Hank, she continued silently, was an exceptionally delightful man. Every date with him was an adventure. But of late there had been a subtle change in their relationship. For a long while he'd been almost like a big brother to her. More recently, though, sex had insinuated itself into the picture, although to date neither she nor Hank had actually done anything about this. Tiffany, frankly, didn't want to. At least she hadn't wanted to until tonight.

Now she wondered if what she needed was an affair with a man . . . and she could not think of a more marvelous candidate than Hank. Hank would always be willing to let her go, she was sure of that, whereas Grafton Emery, she suspected intuitively, would not easily give up a possession once it became his.

But Hank . . . Hank would be as generous about love as he was about everything else, Tiffany sensed. Nor did she pride herself on her celibacy any longer. In fact, she was more than a little fed up with it. But her friendship with Hank was precious to her, and taking the final step might endanger it permanently. Once they'd committed themselves sexually, retreating to the easy camaraderie they shared right now might prove to be impossible.

She sighed, and very nearly reached for the phone.

There was a chance that Hank would have decided not to go out tonight, a chance that he'd be in his bachelor apartment over in Cambridge.

An instant of hesitation was enough. Common sense told Tiffany that this was entirely the wrong time to think about getting together with Hank. Her motivation for even contemplating such a move was obvious. Subconsciously she was trying to convince herself that by bringing Hank into her life she could manage to shut Alan out.

Shut Alan out? To shut out memories of Alan would be a better phrase, she decided. Simply because she'd met Alan in one of the hotel elevators this afternoon did not mean that he was again going to become part of her life.

They were both adults. And they'd both made their own lives—successful lives—since their divorce. In view of this, certainly the Commonwealth Carlton was big enough to contain both of them for the balance of the week.

Chapter Three

Sally Grant looked up at Tiffany anxiously. "Are you feeling all right?" she asked.

This was concern, not curiosity, and Tiffany recognized it as such. "I didn't sleep too well," she confessed.

"Probably a letdown from yesterday," Sally said sympathetically. "It was frantic in here at times, and I'm afraid I wasn't as much help to you as I'd like to have been. Public relations and sales are more different than I'd thought they'd be."

"You did very well," Tiffany assured her, for this was true. Sally was efficient and quick to grasp situations. Most importantly she had tried hard to fill a big gap.

"Oh," Sally said now, glancing at some notes on her desk, "a Dr. Winslow has been trying to reach you for the past hour. He said it's rather important, something connected with the medical meetings, so I suggested he stop by at ten o'clock. I hope that's okay with you."

Nothing could have been less okay, Tiffany thought dismally, and hoped she was masking her dismay. It was with a decidedly thin smile that she answered, "It will be fine."

It was a quarter to ten, forty-five minutes later than she usually reached the office; it was true, as she'd told Sally, that she'd slept poorly. Then, with the coming of dawn, she'd drifted back into a final, uneasy slumber, only to awaken with a headache that aspirin, thus far, had failed to dispel. And it was raining this morning, a steady April drizzle. Ordinarily Tiffany like an occasional rainy day, but right now she was finding this one depressing.

All in all, she was in no state at all to face up to an unexpected visit from Alan Winslow. She took the stack of mail Sally handed her and went into the inner office, every nerve in her body aware that within minutes he'd be walking through the same door.

She had dressed carefully today, knowing that her capacious bright yellow poncho would protect her chic outfit from the rain. Her black linen suit had a slim-fitting skirt that came just above the knee—a length that now seemed too seductive, Tiffany thought with a frown, for it revealed her long beautiful legs and also emphasized the lovely contours of her figure. Her buttoned jacket, with its padded shoulders, was cinched at the waist and flared slightly over her hips. She'd omitted a blouse and for jewelry had chosen a single pearl necklace and matching earrings. The outfit was rather formal, but she'd been thinking ahead to the cocktail party on Beacon Hill she planned to attend late this afternoon, and she had not wanted to take time to go home first and change.

Now she wished she had settled for something simpler and considerably less provocative.

During those wakeful hours last night she'd done a lot of thinking about Alan. She'd faced, among other things, the prospect that he'd remarried. Just because he hadn't brought a wife along with him to this conference in Boston didn't necessarily mean he didn't have one. And she wondered why this possibility left her with such a strangely desolate feeling. Everything had long since been over between Alan and herself, eight years over. True, "erasing" him had not been easy. In fact, it had been the hardest thing she'd ever had to do. Only the passage of time had helped, each year making her that much more able to cope without Alan, or so she'd thought. Now she reminded herself sternly that her days with him represented a closed chapter in her life, a closed book, in fact. It would be absolutely insane to open even one page of that book again!

With her chin tilted at a firm angle, Tiffany took her seat behind her desk. And when Sally came to the door to announce Dr. Winslow's arrival, she was deep into reading a copy of one of the latest hotel journals.

She greeted him casually, and he returned politely, "Thanks for seeing me so promptly."

"I'm glad I was free," she answered, equally courteous, then motioned him to a chair that was placed near her desk, but not too near. She found it impossible not to observe him as he sat down, not to notice that he was dressed very well. His expertly tailored jacket was in a muted beige, the color emphasized by the chocolate brown handkerchief that peeped from his breast pocket. His shirt was stark white, his tie a very vivid shade of pink, this surprising her. Alan, when she'd known him, would never have thought of wearing a bright pink necktie!

He, too, looked tired this morning. There were shadows under those clear gray eyes, and again Tiffany's glance was drawn to the silver hair at his temples. It was with an effort that she controlled her voice to ask, "What can I do for you?"

He frowned, not quite meeting her eyes, and seemed oddly hesitant as he said, "I understand you're the publicity director here at the hotel."

Tiffany nodded. "That's right."

"Well . . . that may make things a bit difficult for us."

Tiffany looked across at him swiftly. "I don't think I follow you," she said, puzzled.

"Our group held a regional conference in Bangor last fall," he told her. "There I agreed to handle public relations for this larger meeting. I had nothing to do with the choice of location, of course. I was told only that the publicity director whom I was to contact on arrival was T. G. Richards. The name," he said dully, "didn't ring a bell, I'm sorry to say."

With her divorce Tiffany had resumed her maiden name. In correspondence she had taken to using initials because she liked the sound of them. She said, "There's really no reason why it should have, is there?"

Alan Winslow shrugged. "It's rather late in the day to get into that," he answered obliquely. "The thing is, our group has some sessions coming up that should be of considerable interest to the media. I mean, there will be stories suitable for the general press as well as the medical press. . . ."

"I would imagine so," Tiffany said levelly.

"Yes. Well . . . I'm expected to act as a liaison between my group and your office," he continued slowly. "So, as I'm the first to admit, that does create something of a personal problem, doesn't it? If I could think of a way to back out of the job I'd do so, believe me. But there isn't one."

"Oh?"

"I said I'd take this on, and I've spent a fair bit of time preparing myself for the things that need to be done. I'd have to have a pretty good reason to ask one of my colleagues to take over at this point."

"What are you trying to tell me, Alan?" Tiffany asked, coming directly to the point. "Do you expect me to find someone else to work with you?"

"Well, I . . ."

"If you do, I'm afraid I'll have to disappoint you," she cut in. "My secretary was rushed to the hospital yesterday for an emergency appendectomy, and Sally Grant, the girl who is filling in for her, has her hands full." She took a deep breath, then added, "I don't have an assistant, Alan, so it would seem that I'm the only person available who can help you."

For a moment Alan was silent. Then, surprisingly, he smiled. It was an impish smile, one-sided. He looked like a little boy caught with his hand in the cookie jar.

Something ached deep inside Tiffany, a bittersweet feeling that frightened her. She couldn't afford to be vulnerable where Alan was concerned, but when he looked across at her as he was doing right now . . .

He said, "Well, then, I guess we're going to have to put up with each other through Friday night."

"Why Friday night?" she blurted out. "You're planning on staying here through Monday, aren't you?"

His eyebrows raised. "Yes, I am," he said. "How did you happen to know that?"

"The publicity office checks the guest registrations every day," she answered swiftly, as if she had the facts about all of the hotel's guests, their comings and their goings, right at the tip of her fingers.

"I see." Suddenly his face was transformed by an all-to-familiar blankness. Alan had often donned that particular expression when he wanted to conceal his true feelings, and many times in the past Tiffany had found it very difficult to cope with.

"Regardless," he said, and smiled again—but this time it was a professional smile, attractive, but totally phony, Tiffany decided. A perfunctory doctor-to-patient smile. "Regardless," he repeated, "you'll only have to put up with me through Saturday morning, at the latest. I can give you our final news information then. The press wants to cover our Friday night banquet, and there will be TV coverage as well. So you may be able to wash your hands of me even before Saturday. In any event, I hope so."

He spoke levelly, but the words *I hope so* stung. Nevertheless, Tiffany leaned forward, determined to maintain her professionalism.

"Alan," she said sincerely, "I'm as anxious as you are to do a good job on the publicity for your group. After all, we've both become adults."

"Yes, we have, haven't we?" he commented dryly.

She saw his well-shaped mouth curve slightly, and to her surprise she caught a glint of humor in his eyes, this only heightening his attractiveness.

Suddenly wary, Tiffany wondered how she'd thought

she could possibly manage to handle having him here in the hotel without any personal repercussions. How could she have imagined that she could handle conferring with him like this, probably on a daily basis? How could she cope with having him here in her office, sitting across from her with his legs crossed negligently, looking so devastatingly virile?

She drew back mentally, as sharply as if she'd been slapped. Unbelievably, desire was stirring within her—a treacherous hunger she'd not felt since the last time she'd been in Alan's arms, since the last time he'd made love to her. She stirred, terribly aware of his nearness . . . and of his body, a body about which she knew everything, from the scar high on his right thigh, leftover from a bicycle accident when he was ten, to the way he liked to sleep on his stomach, one arm outspread to clutch her to him.

She caught the faint scent of his aftershave and wrinkled her nose slightly. The smell was delightfully different and sensual when combined with Alan's natural male warmth. It was faintly spicy and rather exotic. The aftershave he'd used when they'd been married had been lighter, more citrusy. Somehow this was symbolic, the difference seeming to prove that Alan had changed, even as she had.

She saw that the humor had faded from his eyes, and he was watching her closely. There was a husky note in his voice as he asked, "Is working with me going to be too difficult for you, Tiffany?"

"No," she retorted hastily. "Of course not."

Again he was silent, and only someone who knew him very well would have sensed his relief. After a moment he went on, his tone subtly changed. "Shall we set up a time when we can go over the material I have?"

"Certainly," she told him casually, managing to convince herself for just a few seconds that Alan was like so many other men who came into her office seeking her advice on publicity matters. "If you'd like, I can put you in touch with the media people who would be the greatest help to you. Also, it's important not to overlook anyone when it comes to issuing invitations for your banquet, or for any cocktail parties you might be planning. Of course, these things should already have been taken care of. I wish you'd gotten in touch with me sooner. . . ."

"Do you, Tiffany?" he asked, plainly skeptical.

Tiffany drew a deep breath. "It would have made it easier to set up your program," she said evasively. "But there's no big problem, even now." She glanced at her desk calendar and added smoothly, "If you're going to be free around three, let's take a look at what you have. I have an engagement later in the afternoon, but at least we can get through the basics, make a few phone calls, and get things rolling, all right?"

"Fine," Alan began. But before he could say anything else, the intercom buzzed.

"Hank Carella," Sally said apologetically. "He seems anxious. I thought I'd better put him through to you."

"I'll have to take this," Tiffany told Alan.

He nodded, got up and started toward the door. She waved her hand in brief farewell, then picked up the phone to talk to Hank, relieved to be turning her attention elsewhere.

Alan walked down the corridor and back to his own room slowly and let the door close with a thud behind him. The maid had been in to straighten things out in his absence, so there was a pristine quality to the room. Sterile, he thought. But in a different way than an operating room was sterile. This was . . . *lonely*, that was the word.

Like Tiffany's office, his room was in the front of the hotel and looked out over the park. It was tastefully furnished in earth tones, pleasantly luxurious, exactly what one would expect in a hotel of the Commonwealth Carlton's caliber. It really was an amazing hostelry, he conceded. Something like a thousand rooms, if he remembered correctly. The fashionable hotel to stay at in Boston these days, attracting many important meetings like his own, many important people.

Tiffany had quite a job. And there was no doubt in his mind that she handled it very well. Her competency, her smoothness, was overwhelmingly evident to him. She'd become a true professional, and he admired professionalism wherever he found it. Too many people were amateurs at their jobs, getting by and often fooling the public in the process.

Strangely, he had faith in Tiffany. He was certain that it would not occur to her to sabotage his efforts to get good publicity for the upcoming medical conferences because of any sort of personal vendetta. Rather, he had no doubt at all that she would put herself out to do an excellent job and would make sure that no aspect of newspaper, magazine or TV coverage was overlooked.

But could he bear to work with her? Could he stand to be with her for the next four days without even touching her?

Alan walked over to the window and gazed down at the Public Garden. Flowers were beginning to bloom, he noticed wistfully. Trees were sporting an infinite number of tiny green buds. In the distance, atop Beacon Hill, sunlight reflected off the shiny gold dome of the State House. Seeing all this, he realized anew that the city of Boston, cosmopolitan and historical, with its harbor, hospitals and universities, had always fascinated him. He'd been here once before, as a young boy. This was his first visit as an adult—thinking the word made him remember, wryly, his comment to Tiffany—and he wished he could take off and explore the whole town. Downstairs in the lobby last night he'd seen the folders outlining the many points of interests Boston offered. He'd even decided that he would make the time to walk the Freedom Trail, tracing all the famous Revolutionary landmarks. Now, though, he knew there would be no joy in doing any of this by himself.

Common sense told him that as soon as he'd known about Tiffany's position in the hotel, he should have turned the handling of his group's publicity over to someone else. Although some of his colleagues might have protested mildly if he'd done so, the fact remained that there would have been no dire consequences. He'd overstated the difficulties involved to Tiffany because . . .

Alan stood very still, thinking about this. Cautiously allowing himself to complete the thought, he finally admitted that he'd played up his responsibilities because he hadn't wanted to lose this one possible way of keeping in touch with his beautiful ex-wife, now that he'd found her again.

Found her again! Their meeting had been pure coincidence. He'd not "found" Tiffany at all. Even being in the same room with him obviously made her both restless and unhappy. She might as well have shouted her relief when her phone had rung just now, abruptly bringing their interview to a close.

Tiffany, he mused, had very definitely built a shell around herself, at least insofar as he was concerned, but who could blame her? She had a life all her own now, something she'd worked for and created by herself, something he had nothing but admiration for. Still, the idea that he'd never been a part of this, and could never hope to be, stung deeply.

Tiffany picked up the telephone receiver and heard Hank Carella say, "Thanks for fixing up Vernon Platt."

"What?" she asked.

Hank laughed. "Okay, that may not be the exact way to put it. But Vernon really appreciates the accommodations you were able to get for him. I gather he's living in luxury up there on the fourteenth floor of your hotel and loving every minute of it. I can promise you that he'll have some nice things to say about the Commonwealth Carlton on my program, and I won't discourage them . . . much as I normally abhor free plugs."

Tiffany had forgotten all about Vernon Platt since talking to the front office manager about the absolute necessity of getting a good room for him. Once again, she realized now, Fred Bates had come to her rescue, bless him. On the spur of the moment she decided that she'd write a profile about Fred and place it with one of the hotel journals. It wouldn't hurt his career in the least to get some well-deserved publicity.

"Are you there, as our British cousins say?" Hank persisted.

"Yes. I'm sorry, Hank. It's been a rather . . . strange morning."

"Sweet child, it's only ten thirty," Hank reminded her. "The morning's barely half over."

"Nevertheless—"

"Nevertheless, even though this is a last-minute request, I wonder if you'd be free for lunch? Vernon wants to meet you. He suggested we could grab a bite right in the hotel, in the Veranda Room. So can you join us, say at about twelve thirty?"

She didn't hesitate. The chance to meet Vernon Platt was too great to bypass. The man's influence was national in scope, and he'd be a very good friend for the hotel to have.

"I'll be there, Hank," she said enthusiastically, and was glad that she'd worn the black linen outfit after all.

"Listen to you!" Hank grumbled jokingly. "I'd like to think you'd be just as agog if this little get-together involved only you and me."

"And who's to say that I wouldn't be?" she teased, able to do this with Hank, whereas with most men she wouldn't consider such a thing.

"You have a habit of saying things like that when there are approximately ten city blocks separating us," Hank accused. "But if I were right there in your office . . ."

She chuckled. "I know. I'd be screaming for help."

"Tiffany, Tiffany . . ." Hank chuckled too, but when he continued there was a deeper note in his voice, and it held a bit more meaning than she wanted to hear just now. "What am I going to do with you?" he asked.

"Just . . . be kind," Tiffany found herself saying softly, surprising herself.

There was a pause on the line before Hank demanded, "Tiffany, is there something wrong?"

"No. . . . Should there be?"

"You're hedging, beautiful. Something's got you on edge, right?" Hank knew her very well. And before she could think up a suitable answer he added, "How about telling old Uncle Hank about it?"

"Not now," she said. "I have a thousand things to do, Hank, if I'm going to meet you two hours from now. Okay?"

"No," he said gruffly, "but for the moment I guess I'll have to let it go."

Tiffany did have a full schedule for the balance of the morning. She wanted to clear her desk of a number of things so that she would be free to help Alan map out the publicity for the medical meetings . . . and this, she told herself, was something she would have done anyway, no matter who was acting as liaison for the doctor's group.

Shortly before twelve thirty she freshened her make-up and added a dash of her favorite perfume. Catching a whiff of its delightful scent, she realized that this was one of the few things about herself she hadn't changed. She'd used Royal Secret ever since she could remember. She'd been wearing it at Lake George when she first met Alan. She'd worn it on their wedding day, and later . . .

Quickly she put the small flask of the scent she always carried with her back in her handbag and made her way downstairs.

The Veranda Room was a delightful place for breakfast or lunch, deceptively rustic in decor but comfortable and luxurious. The color scheme, fresh yellow and green, white and sand, reflected spring. A verdant oasis in winter, the room was even more appealing now, with vivid plantings of tulips and jonquils in window boxes and fresh spring flowers on every table.

Vernon Platt was a squarely built man with white satin hair, a deeply bronzed complexion and intense blue eyes that missed very little. Perhaps because his personality was so vibrant, Tiffany found him even more attractive in person than he was on television.

Hank's presence would have commanded the best table in the house even if Vernon Platt's hadn't, Tiffany thought, amused at the reception her tall, gangling friend always got. They were ushered to a window seat, and a moment later mimosas were being served to them, compliments of the house.

It was a pleasant luncheon. Both men were excellent companions, their conversation scintillating. There was not a second of "dead air," and as she got up to leave the room with her two escorts Tiffany felt as if she'd been given a much-needed mood transfusion.

She was laughing at something that Hank had said as they wended their way past the other tables, her face alight with the glow she radiated so beautifully when she was happy. Then suddenly her smile froze.

Her eyes were drawn to a table against the wall and the two men sitting there. Feeling herself being raked by the gleam of two metallic gray eyes, Tiffany touched her cheek as if blood had actually been drawn.

Alan was looking at her with a deadliness that was startling, and even from this distance she could see the muscle twitching in his jaw. Then his companion said something to him, and fortunately his attention was wrested away.

But Tiffany's wonderfully lighthearted mood had been shattered. She was numbly aware of Hank's arm at her elbow and felt herself being guided through the rest of the room. Then it took all of her stamina, all of her professionalism, to manage a convincing smile and tell Vernon Platt how much she'd enjoyed meeting him. Platt assured her that the pleasure was mutual, then walked over to the front desk to ask for his messages.

"What was that all about?" Hank demanded.

Tiffany saw that he was glowering at her. "What was what all about?" she countered.

"Come off it, Tiffany!" he snapped. "You went white as a sheet when we were coming out of the restaurant just now. You looked completely drained there for a second. What happened?"

She shook her head. "Nothing happened, Hank. Please, I don't want to go into it."

He looked down at her anxiously. "You're okay, aren't you? You're not sick or something?"

"No," she said, relieved by this tack he was taking. "No, I'm not sick."

Hank's voice was low and replete with meaning. "Then who is he, Tiffany?" he asked roughly.

Chapter Four

Alan and his luncheon companion were emerging
from the Veranda Room. Tiffany saw them out of the
corner of her eye and hoped she wasn't again paling
visibly. Certainly she was overreacting. But why had
Alan looked at her like that? Why had he appeared
so . . . disturbed?

"Hank, you're imagining things," she said hastily.

"No, I'm not," Hank assured her tersely. "Something, or someone, is bothering you. Now, tell me what
it is."

"Honestly, nothing is wrong!" Tiffany blurted, then
knew that if she didn't lower her voice she would attract
attention to herself, very possibly Alan's. She forced a
smile and said quietly, "Really, Hank, I had a delightful time at lunch, but I've got to get back to the office."

"Evading the issue, eh? You use that office as an

escape route much too often. One of these days you're going to find someone's locked the door to it. Then what are you going to do?"

She managed a grin. "I'll just climb up the outside wall of the building and sneak in through the window," she told him.

Hank shook his head helplessly. "Okay, you win," he moaned. And with that he bade her good-bye.

On the elevator ride back up to the tenth floor—Alan had gone off in another direction, thank God—Tiffany was totally preoccupied. She scolded herself bitterly for having agreed to work so closely with him on the publicity for his convention. Somehow, she resolved, she would have to find a way of graciously backing out from this commitment, which she'd made much too hastily. There had to be someone else at the Commonwealth Carlton who could fill in for her. There had to be.

Back at her desk she pressed her palms against her temples, which had suddenly started to throb. Then she nervously glanced up at the wall clock. It was already past two! Alan was due here in less than an hour!

She would have to postpone their meeting, Tiffany decided firmly. That was an immediate and necessary order of business. She simply couldn't face him in her present frame of mind.

She gathered what seemed like her last vestige of sanity and tried to think out all the possible ploys that might enable her to sidestep their appointment, considering and dismissing everything from the timeworn excuse of a sudden migraine to the equally trite ruse of being summoned by the manager on a matter of primary urgency.

Dear God, she muttered frantically. I can't think of a thing. If only Trudy were here. She'd find a graceful way for me to get out of this!

Trudy. Dismayed, Tiffany realized that her preoccupation with Alan Winslow was forcing everything else out of her mind. She'd phoned the hospital earlier and had been delighted to find that Trudy had her own phone. Despite all the optimistic official reports she'd received, it had been a relief to actually hear the sound of Trudy's voice. They'd chatted, and Tiffany had promised to get over for a visit at lunchtime, but she had decided to postpone the visit for a couple of hours when Hank Carella asked her to join him for lunch to meet Vernon Platt.

Trudy had approved of this change, saying that she looked forward to seeing Tiffany later in the day. Now Tiffany realized that this would be the ideal time to pay her hospital visit. Otherwise she might not get a chance to visit Trudy until after the Beacon Hill cocktail party, and that would be rather late.

Sally would be able to handle anything Alan wanted, so she'd simply leave a message, saying that she'd been called away unexpectedly. While this was not entirely the truth, it really wasn't a lie, either.

Feeling as if a heavy weight had been lifted from her shoulders, Tiffany checked the view through the windows and saw that it was still drizzling outside. Quickly, then, she picked up her handbag, snatched her poncho from the closet and hurried into the outer office.

Sally looked up with a smile, then asked, surprised, "Leaving so soon? I thought you had a three o'clock appointment."

"I'll have to cancel it," Tiffany said breathlessly. "Tell Dr. Winslow . . ."

"I'm afraid you'll have to tell him yourself," Sally murmured.

Tiffany turned to see Alan standing in the doorway and felt like a schoolchild caught by the principal in the act of sneaking out. Worse, she knew she was blushing!

Alan gazed at her for a long, appraising moment, taking in everything from her shining blond hair to her elegant black pumps. "It would seem that I'm early," he said, his voice expressionless.

Was he assuming that she was just now returning to her office? Tiffany had no way of knowing what he might be thinking, but she was willing to go with that assumption, even if it meant she'd have to face up to their conference together after all.

He *was* early. Ten minutes early. He glanced, frowning, at his silver-banded watch and said, "Perhaps we should synchronize the time."

Tiffany didn't bother to answer this. Instead, trying to suppress a mounting sense of agitation, she led the way back into her office, thrust her poncho aside and quickly slipped behind her desk.

To her dismay Alan took the chair in which he'd been sitting that morning and moved it closer to the desk, right next to it, in fact. Then he zipped open his leather portfolio and drew out a sheath of papers, saying as he did so, "Perhaps you'd like to glance over these before we get into specifics. It'll give you an idea of what I've done so far."

Tiffany nodded, not daring to look at him, and awkwardly reached out her fingers. But it wasn't paper that she grasped first, it was Alan's decidedly masculine hand. She was astonished at the wave of purely sensuous feeling that surged through her at the mere touch of his skin, and shock at her own reaction caused her to recoil instinctively, as if the contact had burned her.

It was with a sense of horror that she looked up to see Alan's mouth tighten and knew that he'd totally misread her gesture. Deliberately he set the papers down in front of her and then leaned back in his chair.

"Do you mind if I smoke?" he asked.

"No," Tiffany answered automatically, unable to camouflage her surprise as she watched him draw a pack of cigarettes from his coat pocket. Eight years ago Alan would never have smoked. He'd not been a fanatic as far as health was concerned, but he'd had very definite precepts about exercise, nutrition and the use and misuse of the human body. Alcohol had been all right in moderation, but tobacco had been absolutely taboo.

It occurred to her that he must be tense, very tense, to be smoking now . . . and this had a peculiar impact on her. It would be idiotic not to suspect that she was associated with—if not responsible for—at least a part of Alan's present tenseness, and this implied an unexpected vulnerability on his part.

She wrested her attention away from the sight of his lighting the cigarette and exhaling a stream of smoke and forced herself to concentrate on the papers he'd placed before her. Nor could she repress a smile as she surveyed them. Alan had done his homework in typical Alan fashion. There was a precision to the notes he'd made, nothing was out of order.

"What's so funny?" he asked, perplexed.

She glanced across at him. "Nothing . . . why?"

"You chuckled aloud, Tiffany, in case you hadn't realized."

"I'm sorry."

"Look, I admit I'm a rank amateur at this sort of thing," he began, "but . . ."

"It isn't that," she interrupted.

"What is it, then?"

"Just that these notes are so . . . like you," she said, then wished she hadn't.

His expression was quizzical. "What's that supposed to mean?" he asked lightly, and Tiffany felt caution's swift warning. They were on the edge of getting personal . . . and admittedly she was scared to death of this.

"Actually, you've done very well," she said quickly. "I think if you'll leave this material with me I can carry on with it. Your sessions will be open to reporters, won't they?"

"Most of them will be." Alan nodded. He reached over and snuffed out the cigarette in the ashtray Tiffany kept on her desk for smokers. "But you haven't answered my question," he told her then.

"Your question?"

"You said that these notes are so 'like me.' Why?"

Tiffany hesitated, not wanting to get into this at all. She said carefully, "Well, you were always precise and meticulous. . . ."

There was no way in which she could escape the impact of his scrutiny. He said, the words brushed with irony, "You make me sound dull as hell."

"I didn't mean it that way, Alan."

"Didn't you?" He shook his head. "No," he said, "don't try to take it back. I know I got into the habit of . . . arranging things, a long time ago. I took a lot of notes when I was in college, and even more in med school. There was so much we had to absorb, and I tried to find an economical way of keeping everything in order. The abstracts filled volumes all by themselves, you know."

This was an unusual speech for Alan. He wasn't a person who normally explained either himself or his actions to others, as Tiffany knew very well. Now, not only had he offered her an explanation that wasn't really needed, he almost seemed to be asking for her understanding.

"I seem to have digressed," he said blandly, then added, "Anyway, as far as your taking over from here is concerned, I think that's asking too much of you. So I've allowed myself a sufficient amount of free time to work with you."

"That really isn't necessary," she told him, forcing herself to remain calm.

"Isn't it?"

"No, it's not. Only one person can make a phone call, after all," she said, "and when you come right down to it, that's my job." She was determined to get this situation under control. "I'll ask the media people I contact to call you directly or leave their messages at the reception desk if you're not in your room."

"Would it be too much trouble if they left their messages here, with your secretary?" Alan suggested. "My room's just down the hall, so it would be easy for me to stop by now and then to check, if that wouldn't put you out too much."

The thought of Alan Winslow sauntering in and out of her office whenever he wished to was staggering. Yet there was no easy way for Tiffany to refuse what was a simple enough request and a rather efficient solution to their communications problems at that.

"It wouldn't put me out at all," she replied, fearing that her words sounded hollow. Quickly she stashed the papers in the leather portfolio and zipped it closed. "I'll hang on to this, okay?"

It was a clear-cut dismissal, and Alan took the cue. He stood, a tall, well-proportioned man. A tantalizingly handsome man. Yes, maturity did become him, Tiffany decided reluctantly. Even the silver frosting at the temples and the faint lines around his mouth and on his forehead added to, rather than detracted from, his attractiveness. Inadvertently her eyes traced the shape of the head that had once been so beloved to her, then outlined the forehead, the straight nose, and came to rest on the generous curve of his mouth. And the force of her own mounting desire at this point nearly caused her to gasp aloud.

She wanted him to kiss her, to take her in his arms. She wanted to feel his lips bruising hers. She wanted to revel, again, in the tenderness of his touch as he held her and . . .

Alan smiled down at her, appearing remarkably unaware of her reaction to him. "I'll be in touch," he promised, and then was gone with a brief farewell wave.

Tiffany actually felt weak. She heard him say something to Sally, but couldn't decipher the words. Then, after she was sure that he'd left, she got up and walked over to the window, trying to quell the inner trembling that had gripped her so unexpectedly. The rain had stopped, and through the spring-touched trees in the Public Garden she absently noticed the pond where on Patriot's Day—April 19—the famous old swan boats would be put into the water for another season.

Sally would have to fill in from now on, she decided, leaning her head against the windowpane and welcoming its coolness. Sally would have to act as an intermediary between Alan and herself, relaying messages to him and intercepting any further requests for appointments.

Otherwise frequent encounters with him for the rest of the week would be more than she could cope with.

Within an hour Tiffany's determination to sidestep Alan was already being tested.

Sally came to the door of her office to say, "It's Dr. Winslow on the phone, Tiffany."

"Do you think you could handle whatever he wants, Sally?" Tiffany asked, automatically on guard.

"I'll try," Sally promised.

Tiffany tried to get back to her work, but it was impossible to concentrate.

Then Sally poked her head around the door again. "Dr. Winslow says he'd appreciate it if you'd come down to the Ipswich Room," she reported. "It seems he's run into some sort of problem."

"All right," Tiffany agreed reluctantly. "Tell him I'll be right along."

As she rode down in the elevator to the mezzanine, Tiffany warned herself that she must keep careful rein on her emotions in this coming encounter with Alan.

Entering the Ipswich Room, she was surprised to find him working by himself. A long table had been set up at one end of the room with chairs arranged in front of it, theater style. Alan was standing behind the table and fiddling with an array of microphones, moving them from one spot to another.

As she approached he looked up and smiled. And, dim though the lighting was at the moment, Tiffany caught the full force of his smile and felt herself engulfed by his magnetism.

"Thanks for coming, Tiff," he said simply.

It was the first time he'd used his nickname for her since this strange reunion of theirs, and she swallowed hard. Momentarily she felt as if the calendar had been turned back . . . or altered entirely so that time no longer mattered. Tiffany was instantly wary. Alan's use of the familiar name, their proximity in this softly lighted room and the striking charm of his smile were combining to give her some dangerously false impressions.

It took a tremendous effort to remain casual as she asked, "What seems to be the problem, Alan?"

"These microphones," he said. "We're having a panel discussion here this evening, an important one. Some leading cardiologists, cardiovascular surgeons and neurologists as well. We're going to delve into the basic merit of the triple- and quadruple-coronary bypasses being performed almost routinely today. There's still controversy about these procedures and their effects and . . ." He broke off. "I'm digressing," he said. "The problem is that I'm not sure there are enough mikes here, or that they've been set up correctly. I've tried two of them, and I keep getting feedback. Also, I'd wanted a few hand microphones for questions from the audience."

"Anything else?" she asked evenly.

"Why . . . no," he said, slightly taken back.

"I'd be glad to help you, Alan," she continued coolly, "but this isn't my area. Arrangements for microphones and such are handled by sales, not by publicity. You want Robert LeBaron or his assistant, not me."

"I see," Alan said dully. Then, after a long, silent moment, he walked around the end of the table.

Tiffany's senses stirred as he approached her, and, trying not to be obvious about her retreat, she started toward the door. To her dismay Alan followed and quickly fell into pace beside her.

"I'm sorry," he said. "I should have realized that you don't handle absolutely everything in this giant hotel. Which reminds me . . . I had a call from Hank Carella. I've heard he's one of Boston's leading TV personalities. I gather you know him?"

"Yes," Tiffany hedged, trying to conceal her alarm that Hank and Alan might meet. Hank was much too perceptive; he would sum things up much too quickly, given the opportunity. Still, she had only herself to blame for this untimely turn of events. She'd called Hank's office with a message about the medical meetings, true. But she'd assumed that the story would be covered by one of the excellent reporters on his staff, not by Hank himself.

"Carella's going to give us some time on his show," Alan told her now. "He said you'd alerted his office to our meetings . . . and I must say, Tiffany, I'm impressed by your influence."

"It's part of the job," she replied lightly.

"Maybe so, but I think you're underestimating yourself." They had reached the door. Abruptly Alan stopped and placed his hand on her arm, detaining her.

Tiffany stiffened. His touch seared through the black linen fabric of her suit; she felt as if she'd been pierced by an emotional laser beam.

"Tiffany . . ." The subdued tone of his voice drew her gaze upward, only to encounter a pleading expression in his gray eyes that made her feel as if she were being twisted inside. Then, with a hesitancy that was curiously appealing, he asked, "Would you have a drink with me?"

She shook her head automatically. "Thank you, Alan," she managed steadily. "I . . . I'd like to, but I can't. I have a lot of work to finish up, and I'm going to a cocktail party at six."

"Of course," he murmured, still clasping her arm. Then, almost imperceptibly, his grip tightened.

"I know there's no going back, Tiff," he said, his voice low. "And I know that even if there were . . . neither you nor I would want to. But . . ." He stopped and ran his free hand through his smooth brown hair, and it struck Tiffany that she had not seen his hair tousled for a long, long time. Not since the last time he'd made love to her. . . .

"But what?" she whispered.

"Tiff," he went on, "I feel as if you've built a wall around yourself, shutting me out. Does it really have to be that way? Do you hate me so much?"

Hate? Shaken, Tiffany looked up at this man who had once been her husband. Hate was something she'd never thought of in connection with Alan. She'd run the gamut of many other emotions, but hate . . . never. She'd never hated him, she never could hate him, and she tried to find the words to tell him this only to discover that, momentarily, she was speechless. Her voice just wouldn't sound out what she wanted to say.

After a moment Alan said quietly, "It's okay, Tiff." Then, gently releasing her arm, he turned and strode off down the corridor without a backward glance.

Tiffany's eyes remained riveted on him as he walked away, and she found that she was trembling. The temptation to run after him, to make her voice respond again and to answer the question he'd posed to her was overwhelming. But as he rounded the corner into the mezzanine proper, she knew it was too late.

There were a variety of "watering holes" within the Commonwealth Carlton complex. Alan Winslow chose the smallest of the several bars, where the lights were kept very dim. He hoped he wouldn't be recognized by anyone. Just now he wanted to be completely alone.

He sat at a back corner table nursing a Dewar's and water. Impatiently he set the drink aside, lit a cigarette, then a moment later snuffed it out. He returned to the Scotch, taking a hefty sip and letting it scorch his throat, as if the burn it caused would cauterize the hurt that threatened to choke him.

He'd rushed things with Tiffany. That message had come across plainly. She'd made it clear that she was going to avoid further tête-à-têtes with him, and that while she'd do a good job on the publicity for his medical group, she was not about to work with him alone.

The problem with the microphones had, admittedly, been a ploy . . . a stupid one, Alan could see now. He'd hoped to persuade her to have a drink with him, but he'd gone about that in the wrong way too. The suggestion had fallen dismally flat.

He didn't doubt that Tiffany had a cocktail party to go to. He only wondered whether she was going alone or if she'd have an escort. There must be dozens of men in Boston—hundreds of men in Boston, he amended ruefully—who would leap at the chance to take Tiffany out.

The thought that she'd probably been involved with other men came to plague him. But she was a loving, passionate person, and it was ridiculous to expect her to have kept to herself during the eight years since their divorce. Still, the idea of her with another man was excruciatingly painful.

A waiter hovered nearby. Alan wanted to order another Scotch, but he knew he'd better not. Though he hadn't mentioned it to Tiffany, he was one of the surgeons scheduled to take part in the panel discussion that night, and to risk even slight intoxication would be foolish. No, better to go for a brisk walk through the park across the street and then have dinner somewhere outside the hotel, by himself. A steak, maybe. A steak and some salad. He wasn't hungry at all at the moment, but he'd need something to keep going. If not, he would be too drained to speak.

Two men had lunched with Tiffany today, he remembered wryly. And the dark one certainly seemed to be in love with her. He'd fawned over her, Alan recalled, his mood sinking. Personally, he'd disliked the man on sight.

Alan finished his drink and left the bar through a street entrance, then dodged the stop-and-go rush-hour traffic and headed into the Public Garden, walking quickly. Several joggers brushed past him, reminding him of the days when he'd done a lot of jogging himself, both in college and during his first two years of med school. Somehow he'd always found time for a run in those days, and even though the sport no longer captured his interest, he remembered how it had kept him in shape.

Staying in shape, though, had never caused him too much concern. He was fortunate in that he'd never had a weight problem and also possessed a certain stamina, a natural athletic ability and the capacity to fall asleep almost anywhere, given the chance. This had proved necessary to surviving as an intern and resident, although his habitual dozing had irked Tiffany, he remembered.

In retrospect he couldn't blame her. She'd had no way of really understanding how precious, how absolutely vital, those moments of sleep had been to him during the first years of his residency. Nor had he been able to communicate this need to her. There had been so many things about himself and his profession he had failed to communicate, he knew. Tiffany had been young. Too young to realize that although he was deeply involved in his work, she was more important to him than anything else. In his heart, medicine had come second ever since he'd met her.

Today he'd asked her if she hated him. A heavy question, true, because hate was such a heavy word. . . . Yet she hadn't even attempted to give him an answer. Now the implications of her silence stabbed him deeply.

Suddenly Boston seemed to be closing in around him. It was like being onstage in an arena theater. He sat down on a battered green park bench, letting the mellow atmosphere of the enchanting city reach him. There was such a sense of history here. But there was also a sense of tomorrow, especially in his own field of medicine. Today Boston truly could be considered the medical capital of the world.

Thinking this reminded Alan that he should have gotten in touch with Tony Donato before now, yet he was still hesitant about doing so. Dr. Anthony Donato had offered him a position on the staff of the new Commonwealth Medical Center in Boston. This was a tremendous professional compliment as well as an extraordinary career opportunity. Among other things it verified that he'd made a real name for himself in Maine.

Dr. Donato had invited him to tour the new facility— rated among the best of the contemporary medical centers—while he was in town. And Alan had eagerly agreed to do so. But since meeting Tiffany again, the picture had changed radically.

When Tony Donato had asked him to make the transfer to Boston, Alan had not known that Tiffany was living here. Now he had to seriously question whether he could possibly live and work in the same city with her, where she would be at once so near and yet so far away.

Chapter Five

The flowers were delivered to Tiffany's office at ten o'clock Wednesday morning.

Sally Grant was smiling as she brought in the lovely white milk-glass vase filled with pale pink roses.

"Someone you know must really be romantic," she teased Tiffany. "Pink roses always remind me of old-fashioned valentines."

Pink roses reminded Tiffany of Alan. He'd discovered they were her favorite flowers before he'd known her very long, and he'd arranged to have a corsage fashioned out of pink rosebuds placed in the center of her wedding bouquet . . . nearly ten years ago. She'd pressed a couple of the flowers later in a large photograph album her mother still had. She hadn't been able to bring herself to throw out either the album or the dried flowers, but she hadn't wanted to keep them with her. Such things were too memory provoking.

Now she stared at the roses, positive that they were from Alan, although she could think of no reason why he should be sending her flowers.

She saw that there was a small white envelope taped to the vase, and she stalled, not wanting to open it in front of Sally. Fortunately Sally was not an overly curious person. Either that, or she didn't feel she knew her temporary boss well enough to pressure her to find out who'd sent the arrangement, as Trudy would have done.

Tiffany managed to say casually, "When you go down for coffee, Sally, would you bring me back some?"

"I'll go now if you like," Sally offered.

"That would be fine."

Tiffany waited until the outer office door had closed. Then she slowly unfastened the envelope and opened it carefully. Inside she found a card on the face of which a Renoir couple were dancing joyously. This was a small reproduction of one of her favorite paintings . . . and Alan knew this, too.

She opened the card and instantly saw Alan's signature. His writing slanted slightly, and she'd always thought it was not only very distinctive but surprisingly legible for a physician.

Long ago she'd teased him about this.

"Aren't doctors supposed to take a course in destructive penmanship?" she'd asked.

"I flunked it," he'd answered, grinning.

I flunked a lot more than that, the thought came to her now. *I flunked my marriage.* She was startled by this self-admission, as she'd never thought of having divorced Alan in quite that way before. She'd . . .

She was snapped back to the reality of the present when she saw the words he'd written above his name.

Happy Birthday.

Happy Birthday! She was stunned. Incredible though it might seem, she'd completely forgotten about her own birthday.

She stared at the card in disbelief. *Happy Birthday. Alan.* He'd left it at that. He'd not added *Love,* or *Affectionately,* and for that very reason the message came on stronger. It was intended to convey just one thing—after all this time he'd remembered that today was her birthday.

Last night she'd nearly sidestepped the cocktail party on Beacon Hill. After her upsetting meeting with Alan in the Ipswich Room, she'd not been in the mood to socialize. The Brennans, though, besides being business contacts, were charming people, and Tiffany liked them both. Professional photographers who frequently exhibited at the hotel, they seemed imbued with a special zest for life, so Tiffany had decided to trudge up Mt. Vernon Street and visit them after all, hoping their enthusiasm would be contagious.

It had been. Afterward she'd found herself possessed by a nagging restlessness, so she'd walked back to her dance class, something she'd not intended to do. This second decision turned out to be a wise one too. Jazz ballet had been exactly what she'd needed to loosen herself up. The session had provided Tiffany's first real physical workout in several days, and the result was that she'd gotten a fairly good night's sleep. For the first time that week she hadn't dreamed about Alan.

When she'd awakened, though, he'd invaded her mind almost instantly. The expression she'd seen on his face yesterday when he'd left her still haunted her. She hadn't intended to hurt him. Her denial should have been prompt when he'd asked her if she "hated" him. But she'd not wanted to encourage him, either. The situation between them was a difficult one, and she sensed its peril. She was becoming increasingly aware of her own weakness where he was concerned every time she saw Alan.

Tiffany focused on the flowers he'd sent her and tried to sort out a series of varying emotions with no success at all. It was actually a relief when she heard the phone ring on Sally's desk in the outer office. She pressed the necessary button on her own phone and spoke into the receiver.

"Publicity," she said automatically.

"Tiffany Richards, please," Alan said.

"Speaking," she told him, her pulse beginning to pound.

"Well, then," he said, "happy birthday!"

A surge of emotion took over, and it was all Tiffany could do to answer him. "Thank you," she managed after a distinct pause. "And thank you for the flowers, too. They're beautiful."

"I'm glad," he told her, and then hesitated. "I was hoping your taste hadn't changed. Are pink roses still your favorites?"

"Yes," she admitted, then added slowly, "it was . . . very nice of you to send them. I'm amazed that you remembered. . . ."

It was Alan's turn to pause. Then, after a moment, he said huskily, "I wouldn't be apt to forget." He cleared his throat and added, "Twenty-nine, right?"

"Yes."

"And . . . are you serious? Did you really forget that today's your birthday."

"Yes, I did."

"Well," he said cheerfully, "as far as I'm concerned, your memory lapse is all to the good. It indicates that you haven't made any plans. So . . . I'm going to ask you something. And," he added hastily, "please don't answer till you've heard me out."

Tiffany saw a caution flag waving. Hesitantly she said, "Alan—"

He interrupted before she could say anything more. "I'll be free from one o'clock until three," he told her. "Will you have lunch with me?"

Tiffany's pulse fluttered erratically. "Alan, I can't," she began, only to have him quickly cut in again.

"Look," he said, "I did ask you not to give me your answer until you'd heard me out. And . . . well, I admit you may think the suggestion I'm going to make is pretty crazy. But . . . I wish you'd play a sort of game with me. Call it Let's Pretend, if you like. Suppose we pretend that we met for the first time yesterday, when I walked into your office to talk about publicity. Let's assume that somehow I found out today was your birthday, so I told you I'd like to take you out to lunch. Just to have a little celebration."

It was a crazy suggestion. Even so, Tiffany's lips curved into a smile, and her eyes strayed to the pink roses. Regardless of everything else, she told herself, the thought that he'd remembered her birthday and sent her pink roses was touching. Very touching. Taken all by itself, without drawing in any side issues, it was a beautiful gesture.

"Are you still there, Tiffany?" Alan asked.

"Yes, I'm still here . . . Dr. Winslow," she said demurely. "What time did you suggest that we meet?"

She heard the sound of his breath being drawn in

sharply and sensed his surprise—and relief—at her acquiescence. This, in turn, was disquieting and made her think that she should have been smart enough to plead a prior engagement. But it was too late now.

"Shall we meet in the lobby at one, Miss Richards?" Alan suggested.

"That will be fine," she agreed.

The morning crept by. Several times Tiffany was forced to stop working and consider what she'd agreed to. Several times she laughed nervously to herself, thinking that this was really insane. Seeing Alan socially, even if she could manage to pretend that they were strangers, was courting disaster. Though, she asked herself, rationalizing, why should that be? They should both be civilized enough to manage a luncheon together.

There was a staff meeting at eleven, and it dragged on and on. Grafton was in a difficult mood, finding fault with his department heads in a number of small, carping ways. He even reproved Tiffany for something extremely minor, and usually he had nothing but praise for the publicity office.

It was nearly twelve thirty when he finally brought the meeting to a close. The entire session had been a waste of time, as far as Tiffany was concerned, and had kept her from attending to more worthwhile matters. Judging from the expressions on the faces around her, it seemed that the rest of the staff felt exactly the same way.

Robert LeBaron and Fred Bates fell into step with her as they started down the corridor after leaving the executive suite, and it was Fred who said, "Whew! What got into him?"

"Who knows?" Rob LeBaron shrugged. "But I'll tell

you one thing—I'm going to get out of this place for a couple of hours. How about the three of us taking a cab over to Chinatown for some lunch. I hear there's a new place on Tyler Street that specializes in dim-sum."

Ordinarily the invitation would have tempted Tiffany, for she always welcomed learning more about Oriental cooking. In fact, the delectable pastries that Rob was talking about were on her list of foods to try. Still, she shook her head. "Thanks, anyway," she said, "but I already have an engagement."

Fred Bates nudged the affable sales manager. "We might have known," he said, feigning intense disappointment. "After all, with all the handsome young guys who pass through this place trying to make dates with our Miss Richards, what chance would a couple of old duffers like us have?"

"Speak for yourself, Fred," Rob LeBaron growled. He turned to Tiffany and winked. "You'll give me a rain check, won't you?" he asked her.

She laughed. "Any time!" she promised.

The two men left her at the elevator and, glancing at her wristwatch, she realized there was just time enough to freshen up her makeup before meeting Alan.

She reached the lobby at exactly one o'clock, to find that he was already there waiting for her. He was standing next to a large, decorative plant casually reading a newspaper, and he seemed instantly to sense her arrival. He looked up, waved and started across the lobby toward her.

Watching him approach, Tiffany tried to imagine what sort of impression she'd be getting of him if this were really their first date. She studied him carefully, and it was impossible not to like what she saw. He was wearing a pale gray suit with a deep lavender shirt. His tie had bands of purple, more lavender and light but bright blue. His leather wing tips looked comfortably sophisticated. For that matter, he looked comfortably sophisticated.

Sunlight was streaking in through the modern clerestory windows above the hotel's entrance and slanting down across the lobby. A ray brushed Alan's hair, revealing deep chestnut highlights. He was smiling, his eyes very clear, very gray. Surely he'd never been more devastatingly handsome. Tiffany felt as if her throat were about to close.

At her side, Alan smiled down at her appreciatively. "Hello, Miss Richards," he said then, sounding almost boyish. "I'm glad you were free for lunch."

She looked up at him and plunged into the act, hoping she could camouflage a definitely nervous feeling. "Me, too," she said easily. "And please . . . do call me Tiffany."

She was wearing a deep purple dress with raglan sleeves and a scooped neckline, and with it a matching wool jacket. Her slim waistline was defined by a purple leather belt with a butterfly cloisonné buckle, and she had pinned one of Alan's roses at the neckline.

"I'll call you Tiffany if you promise to call me Alan," he said, and then repeated her name slowly, as if savoring the sound of it. "Tiffany. It's unusual," he decided. "Incidentally . . . I like your flower."

Unconsciously she reached up and touched the soft tiny petals. "So do I," she told him. "And as for my name, my parents have offered all sorts of explanations for the choice . . . including telling me that my mother walked by the New York jewelry store while she was pregnant with me and the name became embedded in her subconscious."

Alan laughed and said impishly, "Well, it certainly suits you. Mine isn't quite as unique, but at least it's easy to remember."

"That can be an advantage," she commented with a smile.

"I'm not too familiar with Boston," he told her as they left the hotel and started down the street together. "But I understand that Le Jardin, over on Newbury Street, has pretty good French food. Would that suit you?"

"It sounds great," she said. "And it's only a five-minute walk."

April sunlight dappled the street, its warmth feeling nothing less than luxurious after the bitter cold of Boston's winter. Walking along with this tall, handsome man at her side gave Tiffany a heady sense of excitement. He was so familiar in some ways, yet tantalizingly unfamiliar too.

"Are you from Boston?" he asked politely.

So he really was going to stick to the game plan.

"No," she said, "I'm from New York State."

He nodded. "Been here long?"

"Three years now."

"I don't know too much about your line of work," he admitted, "but aren't you rather young to be publicity director of such a large hotel?"

"Not really," she said, laughing. "Actually," she told him, sobering, "I guess you could say I inherited my job a lot sooner than I normally might have. When I came here to the hotel it was as an assistant to a wonderful man named Mike Haggerty. He was a real pro. I don't think there was a soul in Boston Mike didn't know. He taught me a great deal about my job, about the hotel business . . . and there was so much more he could have taught me," she added regretfully. "He died a year ago."

"Oh?"

"He had a heart attack," she said. "It was a terrible shock to all of us who worked with him. So sudden."

"And after that, you took over?"

"Mike gave me a very good recommendation. When he knew he was going to die, he practically ordered the hotel manager to promote me."

"Grafton Emery?"

"Yes," Tiffany answered, slightly taken back. "Do you know him?"

"I met him yesterday," Alan remarked casually. "He seems like an extremely . . . polished person."

"He is precisely that," she concurred. "Very suave, almost too much so sometimes. But he's exactly right for the job. Being the manager of a large hotel like the Commonwealth Carlton—especially in a city like Boston—requires a unique kind of overview. I don't think you could ever learn such a thing. You either have it, or you don't. Anyway, Grafton is a terrific manager." Except when he's upbraiding the staff for no particular reason, she added to herself silently.

She decided to change the subject. "What about you?" she asked.

Alan seemed startled by the switch. "What about me?" he countered, hesitating.

"You said that you're not too familiar with Boston. Are you a native of Maine?"

"A Maine-iac?" He smiled. "No, I'm not. But I've been at Eastern Maine Medical Center in Bangor going on five years now. Actually I'm from your home state. That is to say, I'm a native of New York City. I did my surgical residency at Albany Medical Center, then

. . . well, I wanted to get away from that part of the country. A good opportunity arose in Maine, so I went. It gave me the chance to follow my particular interests in surgery."

"Which are?"

He laughed. "My interests are rather difficult for even me to define precisely," he admitted. "Every physician is concerned with prolonging life, needless to say. What I'm primarily interested in, though, is the quality of the life that's prolonged. Basically, my specialty is neurology, but this has extended itself into cardiology and transplant surgery as well. Someday transplants will be far more common and successful than they are today. So . . ."

He broke off, smiling down at Tiffany in a way that made her own heart beat erratically. "You didn't ask for a medical treatise," he said then. "Blame it on the fact that I'm subconsciously rehearsing."

"Oh?"

"They've asked me to be the main speaker at the banquet Friday night," he revealed.

"How terrific!" she said, impressed.

"I'm still astonished," he admitted. "I accused some of the older doctors of wanting to see callow youth in action. They tend to look on me as a kid, despite the fact that the calendar belies them."

"Well," Tiffany said judiciously, "you'd have to be over thirty, of course, to be through with your residency and all . . ."

Alan touched a finger to the silver threads at his temple. "To say nothing of having acquired these," he pointed out.

Something flickered in those gray eyes, and Tiffany

felt quick, abrasive pain. It was a stinging thing, and it was also puzzling. Why was it, she asked herself again, that the sight of silver at Alan's temples affected her so strongly? For some crazy reason his gray hairs had a disturbingly personal meaning to her.

She forced herself back to the present, reminding herself that she was about to lunch with Dr. Alan Winslow, whom she'd met only yesterday. She said, honestly, "The effect is very becoming, Doctor."

Alan did not answer her, and for a moment she was afraid that they'd lost the light touch. But then they reached the restaurant and were delighted to find that the warm trend in the weather had permitted the opening of an outside courtyard, a lovely little bricked-in oasis.

They were led to a circular table centered with a jaunty umbrella that looked very Parisian. Alan ordered Cinzano for both of them, after getting her approval, and as they consulted the menu Tiffany discovered that she was really hungry.

First, they feasted on an excellent country paté served with a robust red wine. Then the main course came—a delicious melange of chicken, mushrooms and rice. With this they changed wines to a crisp, chilled white burgundy. There were fresh strawberry tarts for dessert, then cups of strong espresso laced with sugar.

All the while their conversation remained lighthearted, and as they sipped the coffee Alan looked across at her and smiled again. Tiffany felt herself awash in the tremendously potent attraction he had for her. The spring day, the atmosphere, the delicious food and the easy companionship between them—for they'd never strayed from their little masquerade—spelled perfection. And when Alan asked lazily, "What next?" she had to bite her lip to keep herself from blurting an involuntary answer.

What next? Desire came like a torrent, and Tiffany was glad for the diversion when the waitress came to ask if they'd like another espresso. Quickly she nodded assent and went about the business of stirring a spoonful of sugar into her coffee very carefully, trying, at the same time, to fight the knowledge that she wanted nothing so much as to make love with the devastating "stranger" sitting across from her.

He chose that instant to ask, "A French franc for your thoughts, mademoiselle?"

She felt color start to her cheeks and hoped that he was too preoccupied with stirring sugar into his own coffee to notice it.

"They're not worth more than ten centimes," she told him.

"Ten centimes!" he exclaimed. "Even in Paris they would shake their heads at that. Have you been to Paris, Tiffany?"

She shook her head. "No. Have you?"

"Yes," he said, again surprising her. "It was only a brief visit, though, when I was in my third year of residency. I had a chance to go to France with a charter group, and I grabbed it. We were only there for ten days, so I got just a taste of it. But it was enough to make me want to go back."

"I can imagine," she said, trying to take this in stride. She didn't want to be curious, and she had no right to be where he was concerned, yet all sorts of questions arose unbidden. Had Alan gone to Paris with a group of strangers? Or had he taken a companion along with him? A female companion.

There was no need to diagnose the emotion that was gripping her now. It was jealousy. Pure, unadulterated jealousy.

"We'd better go," she said hastily, glancing at her wristwatch. "Otherwise you'll be late for your three o'clock appointment."

"It's a seminar." He shrugged. "I can sneak in after they've started without causing any great commotion."

Still, he called for the check, and with a sense of dismay Tiffany decided that he'd understood her reaction to his reference about Paris, and that this had broken their mood.

Outside the restaurant they headed back down Newbury Street in silence. They had passed along nearly two blocks of fashionable galleries and shops before Alan said, abruptly, "I forgot something, Tiffany."

She looked up at him apprehensively. "What?"

"Well, I didn't forget it, really."

"I haven't the vaguest idea what you're talking about," she evaded.

"Champagne," he told her. I'd intended to drink a birthday toast to you, but then I thought you might want to wait till later for that."

She forced a smile. "It would be the wiser course."

"I wish I could continue to celebrate with you," Alan said, "but I'll be tied up for the balance of the afternoon, then I have a rather early dinner engagement. After that there's an evening conference session I have to attend, so . . ."

Alan was frowning as he spoke, and it occurred to Tiffany that he seemed to feel as if the celebration of her birthday were his responsibility. But then Alan, she remembered, had always given a lot of importance to birthdays and Christmas and other holiday occasions. She had always thought this somewhat strange, because in so many ways he'd been a loner. A popular person, seemingly outgoing, yes. But with a strong sense of privacy.

He'd had no immediate family. When she'd first met him, that time at Lake George, he had told her that his parents had been killed in a car crash in Europe when he was ten. Tiffany had gotten the impression that Alan had been left at home—an apartment in Manhattan— with servants while his parents took this trip. After their death he'd gone to live with his father's older brother, a widower, and this uncle had been on a business trip to the Orient when she and Alan were married. In fact, the only people on Alan's side of the church, she recalled now, were fellow medical students and their wives or husbands.

It was shocking to realize how little she actually knew about him, she thought sadly. Theirs had been the love of youth, and practical things hadn't mattered. They'd been absorbed with their own emotions, dazzled by passion. And obviously that hadn't been enough to preserve their marriage when the going got rough.

Alan said lightly, "I'm about to offer that franc again."

"Again you'd be wasting money," she rejoined, marveling that she could make her tone equally light. They were approaching the hotel, and she stopped.

"Alan," she began, wanting to say the right thing to him, "thank you so very much. I had a delightful time. You've made my birthday . . . special."

"May you have many more special birthdays," he said softly, and before she could respond he bent and kissed her fully on the lips.

Deep inside Tiffany something began to thaw, something she'd not even realized was frozen. She stared up at Alan, her eyes wide, the touch of his mouth burning her lips with an exquisite fire.

It was he who rallied first. "Come on," he urged gently, taking her by the arm and leading her toward the wide glass doors of the entrance. It was only when they were a few steps away that Tiffany saw Grafton Emery standing just under the edge of the huge green canopy, watching them through eyes that were like chips of blue ice. She suspected that Grafton had been headed toward one of the cabs waiting at the curbside when he'd spotted them and had stopped short.

"Tiffany," he said, rather frostily. "And . . . Dr. Winslow, isn't it?" Grafton had an excellent memory for names and faces, a priceless talent for a man in his line of business. He'd met Alan only once, but that had been enough.

"That's right," Alan said, confirming his identity. "Lovely day, isn't it?" he added brightly. "Mrs. Winslow and I have just been out celebrating her birthday."

Tiffany flinched and felt Alan's grip tighten.

Grafton looked quickly back to her. "Your birthday, Tiffany?" he asked politely.

She nodded unhappily. Grafton had certainly picked up on the name Alan had called her, and it wouldn't be long before he'd be demanding an explanation.

Tiffany was right. The call came not from Grafton but from his secretary, during the middle of the afternoon.

"Mr. Emery would like to see you in half an hour, if it's convenient," the woman informed her.

"I'll be there," Tiffany said grimly. There was no

point at all, she knew, in thinking up an excuse that would stave Grafton off. Such a measure would only be temporary at best. And as each minute passed, the fact that Grafton would be doing nothing less than infringing on her privacy annoyed her all the more.

She was in a defiant mood when she entered the manager's private office, which was beautifully furnished in soft tones of blue and gray. The room was a perfect foil for Grafton's own coloring.

"Tiffany," he said, rising automatically and motioning her toward a small armchair upholstered in oyster-and-white striped satin.

As she sat down he returned to his own chair, making a pretense of pushing aside some papers with a gesture that implied they were of no real importance now that she'd arrived. This was another of Grafton's abilities. He had the knack of making whomever he was with feel that they, and they alone, were significant to him at the moment.

"I hope I didn't take you away from anything too vital," he said lightly.

"I was rather busy, Grafton," she retorted stiffly.

"The medical meetings?" he suggested.

"The medical meetings and a number of other things," she told him, knowing exactly where this was going to lead and wishing he'd get to the point.

"Is Sally Grant working out well?"

"Sally's doing fine," Tiffany answered, and then decided on the spur of the moment to take matters in her own hands.

"Grafton," she said, "I am no longer Mrs. Winslow. That was a slip of the tongue on Alan's part. But . . . at one time I was. He's my ex-husband."

Grafton's face was a handsome mask, but she saw

the corner of his mouth twitch and knew he was far more angry with her than he was about to reveal. Hindsight told her now that she should have acquainted Grafton with the role Alan Winslow had played in her life as soon as she'd found out that Alan was a guest in the hotel.

It was none of Grafton's business, true. But as he himself sometimes put it in staff meetings, he liked to run a tight ship here in his hotel. And in his opinion that meant knowing all there was to know about his employees. Grafton was not about to have any breath of scandal touch upon the Commonwealth Carlton if he could help it. He could hardly mastermind the actions of all his guests, but he could certainly keep a watchful eye on his staff.

What a little dictator he was! Looking across at him now, Tiffany almost felt sorry for him.

She stood and said wearily, "If that's all you wanted to know, Grafton, I'll get back to my office. I've got a stack of work I should get through before I leave."

Grafton surveyed her for a long, silent moment. Then he said reproachfully, "You might at least have told me that today was your birthday."

This was the last thing Tiffany had expected to hear.

"I . . . I'd forgotten all about it, to tell you the truth," she said honestly.

"Perhaps you'd have a drink with me later, by way of celebration?" he suggested.

Strangely she sensed that he wasn't trying to be manipulative. And although she wished she could feel angry, she was surprised by the stir of sympathy he evoked in her. It had never occurred to her before that Grafton might be a man to be pitied.

"That would be very nice," she told him.

"How about six o'clock then?" he asked.

She nodded in agreement.

"Why don't we meet in the Pilgrim Pub?" This was the hotel's main cocktail lounge, currently one of the most popular rendezvous spots in Boston.

"Fine," Tiffany promised. "I'll see you there."

Chapter Six

$\mathcal{T}$he Pilgrim Pub was crowded. A table for two had been reserved for Grafton, however, and Tiffany became especially conscious of the way in which the staff deferred to the manager. The smiling waiter who seated them was deferential in a discreet way, yet the impression of homage being paid was there, and Grafton obviously liked it. Tiffany had never realized until now how important such attentions were to Grafton.

A moment later a small cart was wheeled to their table, this holding a shining silver bucket. The bottle inside the bucket was propped up in a bed of crushed ice. Dexterously the waiter removed just enough of the snowy white linen napkin wrapped around it so that both Grafton and Tiffany could see that this was Dom Perignon being served to them. Grafton nodded appro-

val, the wine was poured, and then he clicked his glass
to hers as he proposed a toast.

"May you always be as lovely as you are today, my
dear," he told Tiffany.

The Champagne was delicious. Tiffany returned
Grafton's smile sincerely, for she did appreciate his
having chosen it for her. Yet she could not help but
wish it were Alan she was sharing this vintage beverage
with rather than the man at her side.

As if thinking of Alan were enough to conjure up his
presence, she glanced toward the pub entrance . . .
then wished she hadn't. He was standing there, and he
was not alone. The woman at his side was stunning, a
tall, slim brunette dressed in cerise chiffon. The couple
had to wait for a table, making it all the more difficult
for Tiffany to keep her eyes away from them.

Normally Tiffany doted on fancy hors d'oeuvres. But
now the smoked salmon canapés, the caviar in tiny
patty shells and the other delicacies being offered to her
didn't tempt her at all. She forced herself to munch on
them only to avoid questioning by Grafton, who would
be quick to wonder what had happened to her usually
healthy appetite for things like this.

The moment came when her host reached deep into a
coat pocket to bring forth a small box wrapped in pale
yellow paper. As he held it out to her, Tiffany fought
down a feeling of horror. Certainly he was not about to
offer her a ring?

Fortunately Grafton was in a genial mood again, the
displeasure he'd evidenced at their afternoon meeting
completely gone. He either didn't catch Tiffany's
quick, apprehensive start, or chose to ignore it.

"Open the box, my dear," he urged.

She did so, having just noticed out of the corner of her eye that Alan and his companion were being seated—fortunately at a table at the far side of the room.

The small box bore the name of an exclusive Boston jeweler. But there was a gold charm bracelet inside it rather than the ring Tiffany had feared she'd find there. A single charm dangled from the slender chain. Tiffany focused upon a tiny replica of the Commonwealth Carlton, amazingly accurate as to detail.

She fought back a nearly overwhelming desire to laugh out loud. How like Grafton to present her with such a memento! The hotel was inextricably associated with him. The bracelet would serve as a perpetual reminder.

She hoped that practising how to smile all these months had paid off as she said, "Thank you so much, Grafton. You shouldn't have, of course. But it's . . . unique."

He was pleased. More Champagne was poured, and by the time they'd finished the bottle Tiffany was feeling slightly giddy. She was relieved when Grafton didn't suggest they have dinner together. Evidently he'd assumed that she already had plans for her birthday evening, and she was glad he didn't ask what they were.

As they left the pub she saw that Alan and his companion were still lingering over their drinks. She remembered that Alan had said he had a dinner date tonight. Tiffany felt certain that it was with the stunning brunette. The woman was surely dressed for a special occasion.

Tiffany and Grafton parted in the lobby, and she

took a cab back to her apartment. By the time she got home she was beginning to feel sorry for herself—and there was nothing she loathed more than self-pity.

She couldn't settle on a drink that would go well after Champagne. Maybe some Chablis, later. There was leftover chicken in the fridge; she decided she'd eat it cold, after a while, with a small tossed salad as an accompaniment.

Meantime she changed into a pair of old jeans and a faded T-shirt and got out her mop, her vacuum cleaner and an assortment of brushes and rags.

In an effort to work off all sorts of frustrations, Tiffany spent her birthday evening in a wildly energetic burst of housecleaning.

Spring weather in New England was as variable as a prima donna's moods. Thursday it was raining again, and Tiffany's spirits matched the wet, gray day.

She had been waiting to hear from Alan all morning. She knew that his group was having an important luncheon today, and there had been an excellent interview with one of the doctors in the morning *Globe*. Evidently everything relating to publicity was working out very well. Too well, Tiffany thought morosely. Alan was proving to be very efficient when it came to handling his own affairs. He didn't need her.

She lunched with several other members of the staff in the Veranda Room. Everyone seemed a bit on the down side today; they all blamed it on the weather.

In her office again, Tiffany decided it was time to catch up on neglected correspondence, and she was using her dictaphone when someone knocked on her door.

Sally had gone downstairs a few minutes before to

mail a few things. Tiffany felt her pulse flutter. Certainly this must be Alan, she told herself, and called out a cheery, "Come in."

It wasn't Alan, though. Hank Carella leaned his long frame against the door jamb and surveyed her laconically.

"Well . . . hello," Tiffany managed.

"Is that all you've got to say?" Hank asked, coming into the room and sitting down in the chair nearest her desk, his legs immediately sprawling out to an alarming length.

"What else is there?" Tiffany asked. With Hank at least it was not necessary to put up a front.

"It's a lousy day," Hank observed. "Personally, I have a tremendous yen to get away from the whole damned scene. You wouldn't like to elope with me, would you?"

"Not today, thanks," Tiffany answered. "I'm not very good at climbing down rope ladders."

"Who said anything about rope ladders?" Hank asked her.

"Well, knotted sheets, then," she amended. "People always have to get out of windows one way or another when they elope, don't they?" She shook her head. "I don't think I'd be very good at that. Heights make me dizzy."

"So I'll dig a tunnel, and you can crawl through it and get out that way," Hank suggested.

Tiffany considered this, then said, "No. I get claustrophobia."

"You are a nut," Hank told her fondly, then yawned. "I covered the luncheon meeting that medical group had today," he said. "Just as a guest. I wanted to talk to a few of the doctors before they come on my show tonight. Some interesting stuff. One of these years they'll be taking us all apart in little pieces and then putting us together again. One person's liver, one person's heart, somebody else's kidneys." Hank grimaced. "I think I'd lose my sense of identity," he told her.

"How about trading in an old brain for a new one?" Tiffany suggested.

"Am I supposed to take that personally?" He glanced at the oversize wristwatch he always wore. "I have to get back to the studio," he complained. "If you ask me, the wicked get a lot of rest in this world but there's no time off for the good guys, like me. How about dinner tonight? That's what I came in to ask you. It would have to be on the late side because I'm going to tape the show at six. But I thought we could drive up to the North Shore. I could go for some seafood. How about you?"

Last night Tiffany had been lonely. Very lonely. The thought of having Hank's companionship tonight was a pleasant one. She smiled. "I'd like that," she said.

"My God," he exclaimed, in mock surprise, "for once you've agreed with me. Look, why don't I give you a buzz when I'm ready to leave the studio?"

"Fine." She nodded.

Hank left, and Tiffany went back to her dictating, glad that she'd accepted his invitation. Hank swore that she accepted his invitations on a ratio of about one to twelve, which wasn't far from the truth. This wasn't because she didn't enjoy being with him, but rather because his companionship meant so much to her that she hesitated to take the risk of spoiling their friendship. And this would happen, she feared, if they deviated far from the purely platonic.

She remembered that just a few nights ago she'd actually given thought to having an affair with Hank. Now she was glad that she had not invited him over to her apartment that night. It would have been disastrous, under the circumstances. For she knew now that she was not ready for an affair . . . with anyone. Even though eight years had passed, she'd not gotten Alan out of her system. Their strange reunion had proved that.

The Commonwealth Carlton had three basement levels. The housekeeping department was on the first of them, and lost and found came within its jurisdiction.

Emily Maguire, a lady with fluffy white hair and deceptively mild blue eyes, presided over lost and found and did a remarkable job, in Tiffany's opinion.

Her dictating finished, she'd decided to go down and pay Mrs. Maguire a visit in order to gather material for an article about the amazing variety of things people left behind them in a big hotel.

It was a fascinating experience. Mrs. Maguire was an excellent raconteur and made the most of all the stories she had to tell about the improbable things people tended to forget, upon leaving a hotel.

Within the past two or three months these had included an inflatable rubber vest, evidently stolen from an airliner; one slender glass slipper that could have been used by Prince Charming in his search for Cinderella; a luxuriant black beard, made of real hair; and a golden bird cage containing a stuffed parrot that could be activated by pressing a button and had an extremely lurid vocabulary.

A huge closet had shelves lined with labeled boxes that Tiffany found intriguing enough in themselves.

Some contained nothing but lingerie, this ranging from a wispy bright red bra to a large corset, evidently designed for a very portly gentleman. Then there were cosmetics—for both men and women—covering a gamut of materials Tiffany wouldn't have imagined possible. There were enough leftover medications to stock a small pharmacy, all sorts of reading material, and the half-finished manuscript of something that appeared to be a very bad novel.

"Don't you ever contact people about these things?" Tiffany asked, even though she'd heard the policy on this before.

Mrs. Maguire shook her head. "I learned my lesson in that department back when I was working for the old Boston Statler," she admitted. "One of the maids found this pretty gold sandal underneath a bed, so I sent a card to the people who'd occupied the room the night before and told them we had it. The problem was that the Mrs. Smith who'd been in the room was not 'the' Mrs. Smith, if you know what I mean. What a headache we had over that one! Seems the real Mrs. Smith had been waiting to get the goods on her husband, and he came down on us like a ton of bricks, accusing us of giving his wife grounds for divorce.

"Now," Mrs. Maguire finished succinctly, "we wait for the losers to come to us!"

By the time Tiffany left Mrs. Maguire she felt weak from having laughed so much . . . but it was a happy weakness. She wandered through the maze of corridors in this subterranean area of the hotel and decided to walk up the one flight to the lobby, since she wanted to stop at the newsstand for a copy of the latest edition of the *Globe*.

The staircase doubled as an enclosed fire escape.

Tiffany let the door clang behind her and started up the long flight. She was almost at the first landing when she heard the door clang behind her again. It was impossible not to feel a twinge of apprehension. At off-hours like this there was an isolation about the nether regions of the hotel that was scary.

She chided herself for being over imaginative, but she still had to force herself to turn to see who'd come into the enclosure. When she identified the tall man starting up the steps she nearly stumbled, she was so surprised.

Alan Winslow was equally surprised. He stopped, looking at her as if he couldn't believe his eyes. "What are you doing here?" he demanded.

"I was going to ask you the same thing," Tiffany admitted with a smile.

"I was visiting the printer," he told her as he continued up the flight to join her on the landing. "I wanted to check the proofs for our program tomorrow night. That's quite a print shop you've got. I was impressed. I didn't know hotels were so self-sufficient."

"Big ones like this tend to be," Tiffany explained. "And we're proud of our print shop. Actually, we have so much printing to be done with menus, programs for conventions and special meetings, and so on, that it really is more economical to have our own facility than it would be to farm the material out. And needless to say, it's a lot faster."

"I agree to that," Alan said. Persisting, he said, "Now, what were you doing down in the dungeon area?"

She laughed. "There are two basements below the one you just visited. By the time you get down to the lowest level, you can begin to think about dungeons!

I . . . well, I was visiting the lost and found department. An absolutely hilarious experience, I might add. You wouldn't believe the things people leave behind them."

"Such as?"

"Well, the latest gem was discovered about a week ago—a rubber mermaid, which a bellman found in the closet of one of the suites on the twelfth floor. And would you believe, its long black hair was soaking wet!"

Alan chuckled appreciatively. "Sounds like a natural case for a psychiatrist—if the mermaid's owner can be located, that is," he observed, and then added, in a voice little more than a whisper, "It's good to see you laughing, Tiff."

He was standing very close to her; there was an insidiousness to such closeness. Tiffany started to move up the second tier of stairs, but his arm shot out, restraining her.

She noted that his eyes had darkened—always a danger signal. And his smile had a bittersweetness about it. He said, his voice still very low, very husky, "Tiff . . . I can't get you out of my mind. You can't imagine what finding you again like this has meant to me. To know where you are, how you are . . . well, it's like stumbling into an oasis after living in the world's most arid desert. I've been looking back over these past eight years, and now I wonder how I ever survived them. If it hadn't been for my work . . ."

His work. Instinctively Tiffany tried to move away from him, but his grip only tightened. "Don't misunderstand me," he said levelly. "I worked as hard as it was possible for anyone to work—until sometimes I really did fall down from pure exhaustion—not because of my dedication to medicine, but because I knew it was the only chance I had to preserve my sanity. I kept thinking that maybe the night would come when I could sleep without dreaming of you. When I could get through till morning without remembering the way you'd looked the last time I'd seen you. Your eyes . . ."

Tiffany shuddered. She told herself frantically that she was not ready for this. She wasn't up to handling this brand of raw emotion, she wasn't up to reliving the past or even a segment of it.

"Alan," she began. "Please . . ."

Alan's mouth twisted into something that was more of a grimace than a smile. Bitterly he said "Tiff, for God's sake, don't look at me like that!" Then he added, his voice softening, "Dearest, don't you know that the last thing in the world I want to do is to hurt you? The very last thing—"

"Then please," she said, "please . . ."

"All right, darling," he said gently. "All right." And in another instant he'd taken his hand away from her arm, not to let her go but to draw her toward him.

Tiffany had never felt weaker. Nor did it do any good to accuse herself of having no willpower where Alan was concerned. Just now she wanted exactly what he was giving her. She wanted her senses to be assaulted by him. She wanted to smell the faintly musky, disturbing scent of him, highlighted by his aftershave. She wanted to feel his warmth, to touch him. She wanted to feast her eyes upon him, and to listen as he said simply, "Tiffany."

His mouth descended, and she could not possibly have pulled away from him. There was no resisting his kiss, a kiss that rocked her totally. Tiffany felt herself overpowered by an emotion so devastating that she could not have let go of him no matter how much she might have wanted to, and honesty compelled her to acknowledge that she didn't want to let go of him at all.

The kiss was the distillation of love. Tender, so very tender, and stirring, so stirring that Tiffany felt herself shattered by it, its impact vibrating throughout her body. Yet it was the poignancy rather than the sensuality of it that set it apart. It was a kiss that could have happened only between two people who had shared . . . a great many things.

They parted slowly. Tiffany did not dare look at this man who stood beside her. Her eyes, she knew, would give her away completely were she to do so.

She moved away from him, unable to speak, taking one step upward, then another. He caught up to her, then climbed the rest of the stairs while staying by her side, and they were both silent until they came to the door that opened into the lobby.

Then he said, "Tiff, please, come to me tonight. Or let me come to you."

It was as if a closet door had been opened, and memories suddenly came tumbling out. And Tiffany knew that—potent though Alan's spell over her was— she couldn't risk taking so much as another step forward with him. She couldn't risk loving again—and taking the chance of losing again, as she had before. She simply didn't have the courage.

She shook her head, actually frightened. "No," she said. "No!"

"I'm not trying to rush you," Alan told her quietly. "We have time. I suppose you could say we have all the time in the world . . . if we really want to waste big chunks of it. But—"

She couldn't answer him. She opened the fire door

upon the bustle of the lobby just beyond, and for once she welcomed the noise, the confusion. Right now it served as a reprieve.

It was almost a quarter to eight when Hank called. Tiffany had been trying to concentrate on a currently popular novel while she waited to hear from him and had been failing dismally. She could not blot Alan out of her mind.

The ringing of the telephone was a welcome diversion. Hank said, "I checked, and they serve dinner up at O'Flaherty's, in Gloucester, until at least nine . . . and they indicated that they'll feed us whenever we get there. How about meeting me in front of your place in about ten minutes?"

"Fine," Tiffany said, and it was. She couldn't wait to get out of her apartment; she couldn't wait to put her mind on something else. Hank could not have chosen a better time to ask her out to dinner.

As Hank pulled the car away from the curbside, he said without preamble, "I ran into Emery after I left your office this afternoon."

"Oh?"

"Evidently he knew Alan Winslow was one of the doctors I planned to have on my show tonight. So . . ."

"Yes?"

"You know what I'm going to say, don't you, Tiffany?"

She sighed. "Yes, Hank," she said, "I know. Somehow I thought Grafton wouldn't breeze it around. Not that it matters. Once upon a time, Alan and I were married."

"Just like that, eh?"

"Hank, you've been married, you've been through a

rough divorce. Do I have to spell out for you what it's like?"

He reached over to pat her hand, managing to accomplish this without taking his eyes off the road. "No," he said then, "you don't have to spell it out. Anyway, I knew you'd been married . . . once upon a time, as you say. That's the problem. I put your marriage in a fantasy world, which, I guess, is another way of saying that I evidently didn't really believe in it. Or, at least, I thought it was something that happened back when you were in pigtails."

Tiffany couldn't repress a laugh. "Hank," she pointed out, "people don't usually get married when they're in pigtails!"

"How old were you, Tiffany?"

"Nineteen," she said.

"Young . . . but maybe old enough," he commented.

"What a cryptic remark!"

"I think you know what I'm saying. Some people at nineteen could give the rest of us lessons. Other people . . ."

"I was one of the other people, Hank."

"Yes," he mused. "I figured you would be." He shrugged. "I don't know why it hit me like it did," he admitted. "I had a hell of a time interviewing Winslow. I kept imagining the two of you together."

"Hank!"

"Okay, I have a lively imagination; I admit it. But the guy's handsome as hell—and the worst of it is that he's likable as well. I was prepared to hate his guts, but it didn't turn out that way. Also," Hank concluded slowly, "he's making a real name for himself in surgery.

I was very much impressed by him." He paused, then asked directly, "Why did you divorce him, Tiffany?"

She had not expected such a blunt question. The simple words washed over her like a splash of ice water.

She paused to consider her answer, taking her time because she wanted not only to respond to Hank but also to answer a query that was stirring deep within herself.

Hank gave her time; he didn't try to pressure her. She sensed that he knew as well as she did that what she was about to say was going to be very important to both of them.

Still, she stalled, unable to formulate her thoughts clearly, and finally countered his question with a question of her own.

"Is there ever a single, simple reason for a divorce?" she asked him.

"No," he responded promptly. "But then, I didn't ask you for a simple answer, Tiffany." He let silence take over between them just long enough to let her probe, again, into her own thoughts. Then he said, "If it's something you don't want to talk about, say so."

There was a suspicious roughness to his tone. This told her, more than his words themselves, how much her present reactions mattered to him. She could understand why. If it were still impossible to talk about her divorce, to discuss Alan, then it meant her marriage had not been relegated to the past, as she'd believed it to have been.

She considered this. She'd reacted very strongly to Alan's reappearance in her life. And his ability to arouse her sensually was extremely disturbing. It was a shock to know that he could attract her so much. But, she told herself, once they were apart again, distance would effect its own cure.

Hank had turned off the highway and was driving down a narrow side road. He said quietly, "You've gone far away from me, Tiffany."

It was a more apt statement than he realized. Tiffany wanted to say something reassuring to him, but she couldn't find the right words. She settled for an inadequate, "I'm sorry."

Ahead lay the abandoned wharf upon which the popular seafood restaurant Hank was taking her to had been built a few years ago. Strings of multi-colored Christmas lights edged the sandy parking lot. Tiffany got out of the car, aware of the salt tang in the air and a breeze fresh from the sea. Hank came over to take her arm and to steer her across the uneven ground toward the restaurant entrance.

"Hank . . ." she began.

"Not now," he interrupted. He smiled wryly. "When it comes to explanations about this," he told her, "I don't want to settle for less than the best. We both need a stiff drink first. Maybe a couple of drinks. Then," he added as he held the planked wooden door open for her, "you can bet your last dollar that I'll be waiting with wide-open ears to hear what you have to say."

Chapter Seven

O'Flaherty's was currently one of the most popular seafood restaurants in the greater Boston area. Even at this relatively late dining hour, the place was packed. But Hank, as usual, was given a choice table, and a few minutes later the whiskey sours he ordered were brought over, compliments of the house.

The manager followed almost immediately thereafter. He was an effusive Irishman; any casual onlooker would have thought that Hank was an old friend, Tiffany noted with amusement. Once the man had left them, Hank told her that actually they'd met only once before, and then briefly.

As far as she was concerned the manager's ebullient presence had been a welcome diversion. It had staved off the moment when she'd have to answer Hank's questions.

Now that moment had arrived. Hank placed the

order for a second round of drinks, and his patience was fraying visibly as he said, "I'm not much for making demands. I don't like trying to force the people I like into telling me things they don't want to talk about. But in this case . . . well, in this case, Tiffany, I think I have the right to know."

She toyed with her drink stirrer before she answered him. It was made of red plastic, with a lobster fashioned at one end. She ran her fingers over a smooth plastic claw, then said, "It still isn't easy for me to talk about this. Why my marriage broke up, that is."

"That's understandable," Hank commented levelly.

Tiffany couldn't meet his eyes. She continued to play with the stirrer, and she spoke so softly that he had to lean forward to hear her.

"We got married just a few days before Alan was to start his first year of surgical residency," she said. "I wasn't prepared for what that meant. He did his first rotation in the cardiac intensive-care unit. He was on call most weekends, and on the nights when he was supposedly off-duty he seldom got home before eight or nine o'clock. Then he was so tired that half the time he fell asleep before we finished dinner."

She sighed. "This is going to make me seem very selfish," she confessed. "And . . . I guess it's true enough that in those days I was thinking of myself more than I was of Alan. My only defense is that I was only nineteen years old, I was a bride, I was desperately in love with my husband and most of the time I was . . . totally frustrated. Nobody'd told me that when you marry a doctor chances are that you'll have to take a backseat to his medical career." She shook her head. "No, that isn't right. Alan certainly had no intention of neglecting me, and the times when we were together

. . . and he was awake," she added, with a wry laugh, "it was wonderful. He was wonderful.

"Then," she continued, "September came, and I went back to college. We had an apartment in Albany —Alan was at Albany Medical Center—and I'd decided to commute to Skidmore, which is in Saratoga Springs, about an hour's drive. Right away, though, it was different. Being married, living off campus, put me into a special category. Skidmore is that kind of college. I was no longer one of the girls. . . ."

Hank grinned sympathetically. "I can imagine," he observed.

"Nevertheless," Tiffany said, "things were better once I was back at school. I had my own studying to do; I wasn't quite so lonely. Then, in November, Alan had a week's vacation."

"Yes?"

"We . . . well, we both just wanted to get away from it all for a few days. We saw an ad in the paper for a charter flight to the Caribbean. Bonaire. It's a small island off the coast of Venezuela."

"I know," Hank said. "So . . . you went down there?"

"Yes. We stayed in a hotel that fronted on a gorgeous beach. It was a tropical paradise, and it was also our first real honeymoon. We'd decided that we would not have children until Alan was through his residency. We were young enough to wait. But . . ."

"You slipped?" Hank suggested.

"Yes," Tiffany said, shaking her head at the memory, "we did indeed slip. Too many piña coladas, too much moonlight, no caution at all. . . ."

She straightened, her mouth tightening at the thought of what she was going to have to say next. "By

Christmas," she reported to Hank, "I knew I was pregnant. I dropped out of college at the end of the semester. Pregnancy and Skidmore simply didn't mix."

The second round of drinks had been served to them. Tiffany picked up her glass and sipped, not even aware of the pleasant, tangy taste of the cocktail.

"When Alan found out I was pregnant he was . . . shaken," she said.

"He didn't want you to have the baby?" Hank suggested.

"I wouldn't go so far as to say that, but he was . . . well, he was pretty upset," Tiffany confessed. "Having a child just then certainly didn't fit in with our plans. But Alan was always a person who could take things in stride. He soon accepted the fact that I was pregnant and decided that we'd have to make the best of it. And as for me . . ."

"Yes?"

"Once I was over the initial shock," Tiffany said, "I decided that becoming pregnant was probably the best thing that had ever happened to me. I began to get very excited about that baby. In fact, the thought of having that baby was uppermost in my mind . . . and in my heart as well. My baby. I would have a person all my own to keep me company when Alan was at the hospital. A new life to join with mine."

Tiffany smiled wistfully. "I made up my mind to be the best mother in the history of the world," she confided.

After a moment Hank asked gently, "What happened, Tiffany?"

Tiffany's voice was strained, and there was a remoteness to her expression as she said, "The next August I gave birth to the most beautiful baby boy you've ever seen. The night he was born Alan was on duty at the Medical Center; he was on call in the emergency room; he couldn't get away. He'd planned to be with me when the baby was born."

"Yes?"

"Well," Tiffany said reasonably, "I wasn't the first woman in the world to give birth to her baby without having her husband around."

She favored Hank with a wan smile, and he said, vaguely alarmed at the way this story was going, "Tiffany . . . I don't want to put you through something you don't want to go through."

"Now that I've started I have to finish," she told him. "We named our son Chad, and he was such a delight, Hank. It was such fun to go Christmas shopping that year. Chad would have been four months old at Christmas." She laughed. "I knew Christmas, as such, wasn't going to mean much to him," she confessed. "But I bought a lot of special ornaments for his first tree, and ridiculous toys, and I planned to photograph every minute of his first Christmas Day and to make a special album with the pictures. . . ."

Her voice trailed off, and it was with a visible effort that she picked up the threads of her narrative again. She said, "Chad didn't live until Christmas, Hank. In the middle of December I put him to bed one night, just as usual, and when I went to check on him an hour or so later he was . . . dead."

Hank recoiled, his face paling. "My God, Tiffany!" he exploded. "I had no idea."

"No," she said, "No, of course you didn't. Hank, please . . . don't look at me like that." She tried to force a smile, but it was a dismal attempt, thus making the effort all the more poignant.

She said, "For years I couldn't talk about it at all. I still find it difficult to do so . . . and you're one of the very few persons I'd even consider telling about this. But you're a good friend, and you do have the right to know, as you pointed out. It was Chad's death that broke up my marriage. The night Chad died Alan was, once again, on duty at the hospital. My parents came to the house immediately—thank God they didn't live far away from us—and my father tried to contact Alan. He was involved in emergency surgery, and he couldn't come to the phone. My father kept trying through the night, but he never connected. It wasn't until early morning that the word finally got through to him . . . and then it was three more hours before he could get away and come home.

"I . . . I couldn't forgive him for that," Tiffany said. "Right or wrong, I couldn't forgive him."

Hank asked gently, "Can you tell me what . . . happened to your little boy?"

"Yes," Tiffany said, forcing herself to remain calm. "The cause of death was listed as Sudden Infant Death Syndrome. More popularly known as crib death."

Hank nodded. "SIDS," he said. "We did a program on it just a few months ago. A terrible thing. No one knows where or when it will strike . . . nor is there any way of preventing it."

"That's right," Tiffany said. "There is a National SIDS foundation now, a great deal of research is being done and someday they'll come up with the answers. One good thing that has been proven is that the terrible guilt parents have endured is not valid at all. It took me a long time to believe that, a long time to accept the fact there was nothing I personally could have done to prevent Chad's death."

"I can appreciate that," Hank said. "But what of Alan Winslow, Tiffany? It must have been a pretty rough time for him, too."

"Alan had his work," Tiffany said quietly.

"What?"

"Alan had his medicine," she repeated. "I'm not saying that he didn't grieve for Chad. What I am saying is that he had his work to turn to, he had something else to plunge back into. I didn't."

She looked up at Hank, her dark eyes eloquently expressing her pain. "We needed to grieve together," she said simply. "To mingle our tears. And that didn't happen."

She added deliberately, "I didn't give it a chance to happen, Hank."

He frowned. "What do you mean?"

"I left Alan Christmas Eve," she confessed.

"You *left* him?"

"Yes. He was on call at the hospital . . . and I . . . I packed up all the ornaments I'd bought for the tree and all the toys I'd bought for Chad and drove across to a supermarket where there was a big red Salvation Army box in the corner of the parking lot. I put all those things in the box and then . . . I kept on going."

Hank shook his head, plainly bewildered. "Where did you go?"

"I drove across the country," she said. "I liked New Mexico when I got there, and so I stayed. It is beautiful, beautiful country; the people there are friendly in a good sort of way. They accept you for what you are; they are not inquisitive. I got an apartment in Albuquerque and found a job. Then, after a time, I enrolled in college. I got my divorce in New Mexico, and I got my college degree in New Mexico. I went to work for a public relations agency that had a large Albuquerque hotel as one of its accounts. It was through connections made there that I was offered the job at the Commonwealth Carlton. I was hesitant about coming back East, but Boston seemed a safe distance from Albany. I assumed that Alan was still practicing in Albany, and I had no desire to go back there. My parents had moved to Florida in the interim; I've visited them down there several times. So there was no need to go back to Albany; I felt secure about the whole thing."

"Are you telling me," Hank demanded, "that in all these years you've had no contact with Winslow? How many years is it?"

"Eight, last December," she said. "And, no, I've had no contact with Alan. He tried to reach me through my lawyer, but I . . . well, I wanted to wipe out everything that had happened and to start all over again."

There was a pause. Then Hank asked softly, "Have you managed to do that, Tiffany?"

"I thought I had."

"The waiter's getting itchy," Hank said impatiently. "He's putting the message across to me that if we don't order pretty soon, we won't be eating. Would you care for lobster, Tiffany?"

"Not tonight, thanks," she said, having lost any trace of appetite at this point. "Perhaps some broiled fish?"

"Scrod," Hank decided, and placed the order.

Dinner came, and Hank deliberately talked about other things, casual things connected with his own work, for the most part, which always yielded a store of potential anecdotes. But finally, over coffee, he said, "I can see that Winslow's appearance at the hotel must have been a shocker. You had no idea he was coming?"

She shook her head. "None at all."

"He's still got a grip on you, Tiffany."

"No," she denied. "I was . . . unprepared to face up to seeing him again, that's all."

"Tiffany," Hank said, "if my ex-wife were to walk in here right now I wouldn't blink an eyelash. The luckiest thing that ever happened to me was my divorce. We had a lousy marriage; we were fed up to the teeth with each other long before it was over. I'm not placing any blame. I was no paragon, neither was she, and we came to the point where we were outdoing each other in compounding the errors of our ways. But if she were to come in here right now I could look up and say, 'Hi, Brenda. How's it going?' And there'd be no gut feeling. Do you know what I'm saying? The look on your face tells me that you've still got a lot of gut feeling for Winslow. I can see that it was a jolt to come face to face with him, but if your feeling for him was dead, it wouldn't be doing this to you."

"Excuse me, Mr. Carella," the waiter said, placing two grasshoppers on their table. "These are compliments of the management."

"Thanks," Hank said, eying the frothy green mixture unenthusiastically. He was silent until the waiter had gone a distance from their table, then he repeated, "Do you know what I'm saying, Tiffany?"

Tiffany took a sip of the grasshopper before she answered him. It was cold and creamy, a refreshing concoction, and right now it suited her. Her mouth felt as dry as a desert.

She said, smiling slightly, "I think you're asking me if I'm still in love with Alan Winslow, Hank."

"Not exactly," Hank denied. "What I'm saying is that I think the guy still has a hold on you, and until you get him totally out of your system you're not ready for me, or for anyone else. Not that I'm offering anything like marriage," he added bluntly. "I admit I was burned once, and the way I feel now I don't think I want to go that close to the fire again, even with you. But there is something between us, Tiffany. Call it camaraderie, call it whatever the hell you want to call it. We could have a good thing going . . . if you were emotionally free."

Hesitantly she said, "Your friendship means a great deal to me, Hank. Actually it's scared me every time you get . . . well, everytime you get that lusty look in your eyes."

Hank threw back his head and laughed, a healthy, genuine laugh. "That lusty look in my eye!" he quoted teasingly. Then his voice softened. "Let's take it a step at a time, okay, Tiffany?" he suggested. "I value your friendship just as much as you do mine. Until I got to know you, I didn't believe there was such a thing between men and women as good, honest friendship. You and I have proved otherwise. If there's to be something more—I might better say if there's to be something else—between us, there's plenty of time in which to work it out.

"But my prescription, beautiful, is to face up to your doctor. It seems to me," he finished judiciously, "that eight years ago you didn't give him much of a chance."

Tiffany stopped at the coffee shop in the hotel on her way to work the next morning for a raspberry and almond croissant, one of the shop's delicious specialties. With it she had café au lait, and she was just finishing her second cup when she saw Alan enter the room with the same brunette who had been his companion in the Pilgrim Pub the other evening.

She signed the check the waiter proffered and made ready to leave. She thought of stopping by Alan's table on her way out to say hello, then decided against it.

She was still thinking about the comments Hank had made last night. He'd accused her of not giving Alan a fair chance eight years ago, and though not too long ago this would have aroused her indignation, she had to admit now that Hank was right. She had judged Alan in a very harsh way, she could see that.

This realization made her oddly reticent to approach him right now, nor did she want to interrupt the rather intense conversation he and the brunette were having.

Tiffany left the coffee shop, definitely curious about Alan's companion. There were a number of women attending the medical meetings. Was she one of them? Did she, perhaps, work with Alan? At the thought of this Tiffany could not repress a pang of envy.

Alan saw Tiffany leaving the coffee shop, and he sighed ruefully.

"What was that about?" his companion asked at once.

"I'm getting butterflies thinking about tonight," he evaded. And this, actually, was not a fabrication. He'd never grown accustomed to getting up and speaking in front of a group of people. Once he got into his subject he was all right, but the first couple of minutes after the introduction were inevitably an ordeal.

Camilla Vegas laughed. "You can't be serious," she said. "I've heard you speak several times, remember? I can't think of anyone calmer than you are, and within minutes you have your audience in the palm of your hand—as you very well know."

"I don't know anything very well," Alan muttered, his mind having strayed from the thought of the speech he had to give tonight to Tiffany. He'd tried to call her several times last night, at her apartment, but there'd been no answer, and so he'd reached the obvious conclusion that she was out for the evening.

He'd wondered who she was with and had made a bet with himself that it was either Grafton Emery or Hank Carella. He was sure both men were interested in her.

He'd recognized Carella at once as the man who'd lunched with Tiffany earlier in the week. Fortunately he'd not been next to Carella at yesterday's luncheon, although they'd been near enough. But he'd wished there'd been a way he could have begged out of last night's interview. He'd had the funny feeling that Carella wasn't enjoying it any more than he was.

"How about walking over to Bonwit's with me," Camilla said. "I have a couple of free hours, and I thought I'd try to find something very special to wear for the big occasion tonight."

Alan answered almost absently, "Anything you wear always looks special, Camilla." He hesitated. "I'd like to come along with you, but there are a couple of sessions this afternoon that I should attend. So . . . I'll see you at the banquet."

She smiled. "You don't really have to hold my hand, you know," she told him. "If you'd like to invite someone else to give you moral support, it's perfectly okay. I'll manage."

Alan smiled ruefully. "There's no one else," he said, which, unfortunately, was entirely too true. Although he couldn't help but hope that there might be a chance—even a slim chance—of Tiffany deciding on her own to come and hear him tonight.

Camilla knew how to take this statement, whereas another woman might have read an unintended meaning in it. She was a highly competent physician herself, and she also happened to be married to Alan's best friend, an obstetrician who hadn't been able to get away to accompany her to Boston. The three of them had been in the same class in medical school.

She patted his hand in a near-maternal fashion. "Don't worry," she assured him. "You're going to do fine tonight."

Alan nodded, and a few minutes later they parted in the lobby, each of them going to separate meetings. This was the wind-up day of the conference, and there was a lot going on. Alan didn't have a spare minute during the morning, and it was noon before he knew it.

He went back to his room and freshened up and then strolled down the hall to the publicity office. Tiffany's secretary was at her desk, but he saw that the door to Tiffany's office was wide open, and he was disappointed. He'd hoped to persuade her to have a sandwich with him here in the hotel, since he didn't have time to go out. But any sort of crumb, he thought—wincing slightly at the pun—would be preferable to not seeing her at all.

"Hello, there, Dr. Winslow," Sally Grant said cheerfully. "Can we do something for you?"

The *we* was gratuitous. He forced a smile. "I was looking for Miss Richards," he confessed, stumbling slightly over the name and nearly saying "Mrs. Winslow" again. "There were a couple of things I wanted to talk to her about. Nothing . . . urgent," he added.

Sally looked properly regretful. "Miss Richards had

a luncheon appointment outside the hotel," she reported. "She said she'd be back around two. Could she call you when she comes in?"

Alan shook his head. "No," he said. "It's all right . . . nothing that won't take care of itself, I'm sure. I'll catch up with her later."

But would he, he wondered?

Chapter Eight

$\mathcal{T}$iffany was lunching with Trudy Barnes. Trudy had called during the middle of the morning to reveal that she'd just been released from the hospital and was back at her apartment on Marlborough Street, in the Back Bay.

"Do you have someone staying with you?" Tiffany had asked instantly.

"No, but I don't need anyone," Trudy had insisted with the confidence that was such a trademark of hers. "I could come back to work tomorrow."

"That's what you think," Tiffany had said firmly. "I'm not having you darken my door until you're one hundred percent fit again, Trudy." She paused. "I'd like to darken yours, though, if that's all right with you. How about my coming for lunch if I bring the lunch with me?"

"You can come even if you don't bring the lunch with you," Trudy had rejoined promptly, delighted at the idea.

Tiffany had left her office about fifteen minutes before Alan Winslow paid his visit to it. She walked the eight long blocks over to Trudy's apartment, pausing at a deli on the way, where she bought an assortment of cold cuts, some Jewish rye bread and two or three different kinds of cheese. At the last minute she also splurged on some succulent macaroon tarts that looked too good to resist.

Trudy was pale, and she moved rather cautiously, but her smile was radiant, and Tiffany didn't know when she'd been so glad to see someone.

"I can't believe it was only last Monday that you went to the hospital," she said, surveying this secretary who was also such a good friend. "It seems as if you've been away ten years."

"Has the work load been that bad without me there to handle things?" Trudy teased.

"Bad enough. But I wasn't thinking of the work load."

"Oh?"

"Look, sit down, will you?" Tiffany implored, for Trudy was taking the food out of brown paper bags and admiring it as she set it on a counter. "I'll take care of everything. Matter of fact, you should probably be in bed, shouldn't you?"

"No," Trudy said. "I'm supposed to move around. I just have to be sensible, that's all. I'll take a nap this afternoon."

"You, sensible?" Tiffany scoffed. But actually Trudy was one of the most sensible people she knew. She very much admired the way Trudy had handled her own life.

She'd married her high school sweetheart, the son of a fairly prosperous lumberyard owner, in their hometown in western Massachusetts. Her husband had been blatantly unfaithful; finally it was he who asked Trudy for a divorce. It had been a bitter business, but afterward Trudy had picked up the pieces and had moved to Boston, enrolling in a business college. Eventually she'd found her niche in life as an executive secretary. She was excellent at her job, as Tiffany had discovered during those first weeks after Mike's death, when she'd inherited Trudy with the publicity office. In fact, Trudy's expertise was one reason why she hadn't been more arduous about seeking an assistant publicity director. The two of them worked so well together. She wanted to be very careful before she let a third person in.

Trudy brushed back a dark red curl now and sat down carefully on the nearest chair, wincing slightly. Noticing Tiffany's concerned glance she said, "The incision's still sore."

"Any dietary restrictions?" Tiffany thought to ask.

"None."

"Okay, then. How about a glass of burgundy?"

"Sounds ambrosial."

Tiffany poured wine for both of them, and they drank a toast to each other. Then she put her glass aside and set about making the sandwiches. She felt herself relaxing here in Trudy's small apartment. She was only beginning to realize just how tense she'd been all week.

They munched for a time; then, without preamble, Trudy said, "Well? Out with it!"

"Out with what?" Tiffany asked innocently.

"What's been going on? I thought I looked like I'd

been put through an endurance test when I glanced in the mirror this morning, but you more than match me."

"Is it that obvious?" Tiffany asked ruefully.

"Yes! Now, tell Mother Trudy what's been happening in her absence. Has Grafton declared himself?"

"Oh, my God!" Tiffany laughed helplessly and then couldn't refrain from detailing her experience with Grafton on her birthday, when he'd first plied her with Dom Perignon and then given her the little jewelry box which, she'd feared, would contain a ring.

"And you're telling me he gave you a charm that's a replica of the hotel?" Trudy demanded incredulously, then nearly doubled up with laughter only to immediately straighten and say, "Ouch! Look, let's keep this conversation more serious, shall we? Also, how about some more wine? It's good to ease the pain."

Tiffany refilled their glasses, then she said thoughtfully, "You know . . . I've actually begun to feel rather sorry for Grafton, Trudy. I suspect that he'd turn and run a mile if I began to take his attentions seriously. I think what he really wants is . . ."

She bit her lip, because the statement she was about to make gave an implication of conceit she didn't intend. But, as she often did, Trudy second-guessed her.

"Grafton likes to be seen with young, beautiful women who make him feel as if he's twenty years younger than he is," Trudy said astutely. "That's what you were about to say, isn't it? Well, you're right, Tiffany. From what I've heard, I think he had a sterile sort of marriage. His wife was rather formidable—I know people who knew her. On the board of all sorts of charities, a club woman, you know the type. Also, she held the purse strings. Once she died, Grafton came into his own, and I understand he really blossomed. Then he was offered the job of manager at the Commonwealth Carlton, and I have to hand it to him. He's made the hotel the talk of Boston. It's the in place right now; there's no doubt of it. Much of that is due to Grafton's talent for manipulating . . . all sorts of things. But on the personal level . . . well, to tell you the truth I don't think he's all that sexy, Tiffany. He has to come on like God's gift to women to keep his own ego in good repair, that's all."

"You're impossible, Trudy!" Tiffany sputtered.

"Maybe. But I suspect you've had more than Grafton on your plate this week, haven't you?" Trudy guessed.

"Yes," Tiffany admitted. And in another minute she was telling Trudy about meeting Alan in the elevator . . . and most of the things that had been happening since.

By the time she'd finished recounting the episodes involving Alan, and telling Trudy about her dinner date with Hank Carella the previous evening as well, it was nearly two o'clock, but Tiffany had no desire at all to leave this warm little apartment or Trudy's companionship.

She sighed and said reluctantly, "I'll have to get back to work."

"This is the last day for the medical group, isn't it?" Trudy asked.

"Yes. They're having their banquet tonight. Alan is the principal speaker."

"Are you going?"

"I doubt it. Not to the dinner. But—"

"I'd lay bets that you can't keep yourself from going to hear him speak," Trudy said bluntly.

"You'd have to lay them with someone else," Tiffany rejoined, and admitted, "I'm afraid I might lose."

"Tiff," Trudy said, and Tiffany stiffened. Trudy was the only other person who sometimes used Alan's nickname for her. "Tiff, are you still in love with your ex-husband?"

"That's such a leading question," Tiffany protested.

"I suppose it is. But . . . look, I admit this comes as a surprise to me," Trudy said. "I thought your marriage had been relegated to the past as much as mine has been. And, believe me, if Clement Barnes were to walk in here right now, my pulse wouldn't even flutter. I'll never forget the way I felt the day I got the final decree. Free. Free as birds are supposed to be. In fact I felt like I'd sprouted wings and could fly up and over the whole city. How did you feel when you got your decree, Tiffany?"

Tiffany considered this. And remembered, too acutely, the sensation of loss that had accompanied the knowledge that she was now supposedly "free." It had been a bad day. She'd gone out to dinner with friends in Albuquerque and had deliberately had too much to drink. Fortunately they had been good friends. They'd taken her home and put her to bed and nothing had ever been said about it.

"Your face tells the story," Trudy said now. "If you ask me, I don't think you've ever gotten him out of your system."

Tiffany shook her head, wanting to protest, yet knowing that were she to do so her statement would only fall flat. "You're not the first person who's told me that," she admitted.

"Who else?" Trudy demanded.

"Hank Carella. I had dinner with him last night.

Grafton had told him that Alan and I had been married. You know Hank. Once he gets on the track of a story nothing stops him. In this instance, he felt he had the right to know—and I had to agree."

"So you told him . . . everything?" Trudy asked.

"Yes. Yes, even about Chad," Tiffany said slowly, and was aware of Trudy's surprise. Trudy was one of the very few people in whom Tiffany had ever confided about Chad.

"It isn't serious with you and Hank, is it?" Trudy asked now.

Tiffany smiled reprovingly. "You've just said you think I'm still carrying the proverbial torch for my ex-husband," she reminded her secretary.

"Even so."

"Even so." Tiffany nodded. "No, it isn't serious with Hank and me," she said then. "We're friends, very good friends. Last night did establish that. I think we both know where we stand, now, and will be more comfortable with each other because of it. He's a terrific person. . . ."

She paused; something had suddenly struck her. The urge to play matchmaker! Why hadn't she ever seen it before? Hank and Trudy would be perfect for each other.

All the way back to the hotel she was thinking about this. Trudy and Hank had met, of course, many times, but against the background of the publicity office. Tiffany was certain they'd never really looked at each other. And she was going to have to see to it that before much longer they did exactly that!

Tiffany seldom attended any of the banquets given in the hotel. There were so many of them, for one thing.

And even though most groups made the gesture of sending the publicity director an invitation, she'd always assumed that this was mainly a token thing.

Tonight, though, she found it impossible to stay away from the grand ballroom, where Alan would be speaking. Probably, she thought whimsically, she wouldn't understand five words he said. Nevertheless, she wanted to hear him; she wanted to see him; she wanted to listen to the sound of the applause that would be for him.

She went home around five o'clock and had an early supper. Then she rested for a while. She'd intended taking a nap, but it was impossible to get to sleep.

She wanted to look her best that night. True, there was a chance Alan might not even see her, as she planned to find a seat in the back of the room. She had no intention of deliberately trying to attract his attention. Nevertheless, she wanted to look really terrific.

She decided to wear one of her favorite outfits for evening. The dress was white chiffon, made with petal cap sleeves, a fitted waist and a full skirt. The high, round neck was studded with pearl buttons that extended down the front to the waist. It was a lovely dress, setting off Tiffany's blond beauty perfectly. With it she wore shimmering silver stockings and high heeled white shoes with narrow straps.

She was surprised at the crowd in the grand ballroom. A major part of Boston's medical fraternity must have decided to come to hear Alan, she decided, in addition to the conference participants themselves. She edged her way into the last row of chairs trying to be as inconspicuous as possible, then saw that Alan was being introduced by an elderly white-haired doctor.

She sat forward on the edge of the seat, hanging on

this man's words. He was really lauding Alan. And although once she'd resented the role medicine had played in Alan's life—and in their marriage—now Tiffany felt a surge of pride as she listened.

Then the microphone was turned over to Alan, and he stood before it for a moment, not saying anything at all. It seemed to Tiffany that his eyes were sweeping the room, until they came to rest on her.

He recognized her, even at the considerable distance that separated them, and in spite of the crowd. Her hand went to her throat as she met his gaze. It was in that moment that she faced up to the truth.

She loved him.

Hank and Trudy were both right. She never had gotten over Alan Winslow. She'd fallen in love with him on a summer day when she was nineteen, and she would love him until she died.

It was a revelation—a revelation she was not at all prepared for. She was so stunned that she didn't even hear Alan's opening remarks. Or at least his words made no sense to her.

Then, as he continued to speak, she focused on what he was saying, and she became totally captivated. There was nothing esoteric in the way Alan was discussing his work. Rather, he was inviting his audience to share it with him, couching the description of his medical experiences in non-scientific words easily understandable to the laymen in his audience.

Further, there was such hope in what he said. He painted a breathtaking picture of the advances being made in medicine, going briefly into the transplant field, which, Tiffany already knew, was of especial interest to him.

Alan was not falsely humble. But there was a modesty about him as he spoke that was very affecting. It made him seem even younger than he was, and one could not help but marvel at how far this youthful doctor had come in his chosen profession in such a short time.

When he finished, Tiffany got to her feet with the rest of the audience, clapping as enthusiastically as anyone, and loving the sound of the applause that was ringing from wall to wall in the big room.

Well-wishers pressed forward to congratulate Alan, and he was soon lost from view in a maze of people. But as far as Tiffany was concerned, this was just as well. She had no intention of talking with him tonight.

She edged back toward the rear door she'd entered by and had almost reached it when a familiar voice halted her.

"Tiffany!"

She turned to see Hank Carella making his way toward her. Surprised, as she'd not expected Hank to cover the banquet personally, she stepped back to let others go ahead of her and waited for him. They both moved back in order not to block the exit. Hank stared down at her, looking tall and lean tonight, and almost saturnine.

"Pretty terrific, wasn't he?" he asked. "Aren't you going to go up and congratulate him?"

Tiffany glanced toward the head table. Alan was still at the speaker's stand, and he was being mobbed as people continued to press forward to talk to him.

She shook her head. "I don't think so," she said. "Too much of a traffic jam."

She was aware that Hank was eying her closely, and now he suggested abruptly, "Let's go down to the Atlantic Room." The Atlantic Room was the hotel's famous supper club, often featuring top-notch entertainers. And there was always a good orchestra for dancing.

"I'm not in the mood for it," Tiffany said frankly.

"And I'm not about to let you go home alone," Hank told her. "You're not in the mood for that, either, though I'm not sure you know it."

"Have you turned into a mind reader, Hank?" she demanded, exasperated.

"Pettishness doesn't become you, beautiful," he answered. "Come along."

He still had hold of her arm, so there wasn't much she could do except follow along, unless she wanted to make a scene by breaking his clasp. And this, she suspected, wouldn't be easy.

The elevator was packed with people. There was no opportunity to say anything at all to Hank without being overheard by all too many ears. The car came to a stop at the lobby level, and Hank, still holding on to her, propelled her along the side corridor that led to the Atlantic Room.

The head waiter, standing just inside the door, spotted Tiffany immediately. He was very French, and he bowed slightly as he said, "What an unexpected pleasure, Miss Richards. We do not see enough of you. I have just the table for you and Mr. Carella."

"Something in a corner, please, Andre?" Tiffany suggested.

"But I have just the thing for you right next to the dance floor," he protested. "Our floor show is excellent this week. You will want the best view of it."

Tiffany smiled. She'd written an article about this room when it had first opened. An advantage of the way it had been designed was that one had a good view of the stage—in this case the dance floor—from any table in the place.

"A relatively remote corner will be fine, Andre," she repeated, and then knew she'd given the head waiter entirely the wrong impression as he smiled understandingly. For a long time she'd suspected that Andre "fed" scraps of information to the various news sources. More likely than not there'd be a mention of her name coupled with Hank Carella's in one of the area gossip columns over the next few days.

Once they were seated, and after Andre had left them and Hank had placed a drink order with their waiter, she said apologetically, "I'm sorry, Hank. Obviously I led Andre to draw entirely the wrong conclusions. We're apt to wind up in print."

Hank laughed. "I'd be flattered to have my name coupled with yours," he said lightly. "Tiffany, don't look so damned serious about it. Nobody believes that kind of junk!"

"Don't they?"

"No one who knows either of us, certainly, or whose opinions we would care about," he said. "And it might not be such a bad idea if it came out publicly that there might be some romance brewing between the two of us."

"Hank!"

"Please, beautiful, wipe that righteous look off your face! I'm thinking of your own interests!"

Tiffany first addressed the delicious brandy alexander the waiter placed before her. Then she asked, "Are you telling me, by any chance, that I should try to make Alan jealous?"

"It's an old ploy," Hank admitted. "But frequently it's a successful one."

"It wouldn't be in this case," Tiffany said. "Anyway, Alan will be back in Maine by the time anything gets into the paper about us—if, that is, anything does. We may both be jumping to conclusions where Andre is concerned."

"I doubt it," Hank said dryly. "But I also don't think it's the most important thing in the world at the moment." He shrugged slightly, then said, "Again, I have to say to you that Winslow was pretty terrific tonight."

"Yes, he was," Tiffany admitted.

"Tiffany . . . in my opinion your ex-husband is an unusual man. He has already made tremendous strides in his profession in a very short time. But I would also say that he's a very lonely man," Hank added to her surprise. "Those were the vibes I got when I interviewed him. He seems to me like a man who thinks he's lost something irretrievable . . . and is doing the best he can with his life despite this."

Hank paused to take a sip of his drink, and Tiffany, forcing a laugh, said, "Hank, you sound as if you've acquired a crystal ball."

But her attempt at humor fell flat. One of Hank's talents was his ability to read people, to bring them out of themselves; she'd known this for a long time. He was an excellent judge of character. And although she wished she could brush aside his analysis of Alan, she knew that mere wishing would not negate what he'd just told her.

Almost irritated now, he said, "I don't know why the hell I'm trying to play Cupid. But all I have to say to you, Tiffany, is . . . well, give him a chance, that's all. Don't shut him off."

She smiled ruefully. "I doubt it's going to be a

question of my shutting Alan off, Hank," she said. "The medical meetings are over; most of the doctors will be checking out in the morning. True, Alan is registered through Monday, so I suppose he still intends to stay in Boston till some time on Tuesday. But he certainly wouldn't have booked the extra day unless he had definite reasons for doing so. He must have plans."

"So?" Hank interrupted.

"What I'm saying is that I don't intend to go in to my office tomorrow. I never go in on Saturday, unless there's a specific reason for doing so, you know that. The publicity office is always closed on Sunday. So, if Alan is busy Monday, there's a good chance I won't be seeing him again."

"I wouldn't bet on that," Hank said softly.

The orchestra had been taking a break when Tiffany and Hank arrived. Now Tiffany watched them file in and take their places at the rear of the highly polished dance floor. She glanced at her watch. It was a quarter to eleven. The late floor show went on in fifteen minutes, and she wanted to be out before then. She was tired, not at all in the mood for the revue that was being featured.

"If you don't object," she said to Hank, "I'd like to leave before the show begins."

To her surprise he shook his head. "I haven't caught the show yet, and every night next week is full for me," he told her. "I'd like to stay on for it, if you wouldn't mind too much."

"No, of course I don't mind," she said, and added, "I can get a cab."

"Oh, for God's sake, Tiffany," Hank said irritably, and she looked across at him, surprised. "You know I wouldn't stay here and watch the show and let you go home by yourself."

"Hank—"

"Come on, beautiful, don't protest. You know me better than that. What I'm asking is that you have another drink and watch it with me. You could do with a little levity in your life at the moment."

"I—" Tiffany began, but she got no further.

Hank was glancing toward the door of the supper club, and to her surprise he beckoned to their waiter, who was standing nearby, and said, "Will you tell Andre that we'd be happy to have Dr. Winslow and his companion join us? They're waiting for a table; she's wearing yellow."

Tiffany, shocked, was about to say something to the waiter herself when Hank placed his hands over hers in a gesture that was very definitely one of command.

"The place is full," he told her, "in case you haven't noticed. This table is usually used for four; it's only because you get such special attention around here that it was given to us."

"I get special attention?" she sputtered. "You know who commands the best tables in Boston."

"Okay," he said, laughing. "It doesn't really matter. I thought it would only be polite to ask Dr. Winslow to share our space with us, Tiffany. Please stop looking at me as if you could murder me."

"But I could!" she said. "Hank, how could you possibly—"

"Later, beautiful," he told her in an exaggerated whisper. "I would say that the doctor and his companion have decided to accept our invitation. Andre is leading the way, and they're following. Now come on, Tiffany. Smile."

Chapter Nine

$\mathcal{T}$his is very kind of you," Alan Winslow said politely. "Tables are at a premium in here tonight, and I appreciate your letting us share yours."

Tiffany realized that he was addressing both Hank and herself, and she was tempted to come right out and say that the table-sharing idea had been entirely Hank's. But she merely forced a smile.

Alan said to the woman at his side, "Camilla, I think you met Mr. Carella the other day at lunch."

"Yes." The brunette nodded.

"Dr. Vegas," Hank murmured politely.

"And this is Miss Richards," Alan continued. "She's publicity director here at the Commonwealth Carlton."

Camilla Vegas acknowledged the introduction with a smile, and Tiffany managed to smile back, meanwhile fighting the grip of something she had to identify as jealousy.

Alan held a chair for the lovely doctor, and she slipped into it gracefully. The waiter hovered solicitously while Alan placed drink orders for his companion and himself, and Hank, without consulting Tiffany, ordered another round of brandy alexanders.

The orchestra had begun to play; the lights were dimmed; a spotlight was beamed to the center of the dance floor, and a man in a white satin tuxedo walked into its circle.

The floor show started, and it was excellent. The dancers were superb, as was the acrobatic team from Germany. Then the comedians followed, and they were hilarious. Tense though she was, Tiffany was moved to laughter by some of their jokes.

The show closed with a sultry, adagio type of dance between a man and woman who were flawless in their performance. There was a sensuality to their movements that was very evocative, and Tiffany found herself wanting to look at Alan, to meet his eyes. It took all of her willpower not to do so.

The dance ended, and the entire room was, briefly, plunged into darkness. Then the lights around the dance floor came on, and the performers took their bows as applause thundered. The orchestra struck up for dancing.

Almost immediately Alan turned toward Tiffany and asked, "May I have the pleasure?"

It was impossible to think of a spur-of-the moment excuse. In fact, Hank was already standing and drawing out her chair for her.

The tables were terraced; short flights of two or three steps led down from them to the dance floor. Tiffany preceded Alan, but she was so overwhelmingly conscious of his closeness just behind her, that she stumbled on the first series of steps. Immediately his arm reached out and gripped her elbow, holding her until she steadied. Only then, slowly, did he let go of her.

Her cheeks were flaming. She was thankful that the lights were turned low. Those dancing were bathed in rainbow hues that played across the surface of the dance floor in sweeping waves of color.

Tiffany, at the edge of the highly polished floor, pulled back. It seemed impossible to her that she could go on with this dance. She felt as if she would dissolve if Alan so much as touched her; she felt as if she would actually crumble into his arms, all her defenses down, her emotions woefully obvious.

She was trembling inwardly, and she was afraid she'd soon be shaking all over. But then Alan gently drew her toward him, and in another moment they were gliding out onto the floor, dancing in what Alan, years ago, had called, "the old-fashioned way," because this number was a waltz.

He had always been a very good dancer, and they'd always moved well together, she following his lead effortlessly no matter how intricate his steps. Many times, in the past, they'd wound up having the floor all to themselves, the other dancers going to the sidelines to watch them. Tiffany was determined now that even if she had to become deliberately awkward and step on his feet that wasn't going to happen this time. She was sure she couldn't stand being the center of such attention tonight.

Alan had not yet said a word to her. Gradually she found herself relaxing, because that was the effect music had on her. It was the one thing in the world guaranteed to ease her tensions, to force her to unknot.

And it seemed so right, being in his arms, dancing with him again. Tiffany, responding both to the music and to this devastating man holding her so easily, suddenly felt that nothing mattered except this moment. Nothing at all.

This was the only moment upon which she could count. The present. The tangible reality of being here, now, with Alan. Inevitably the present would soon become past, and the future would loom ahead, unpredictable as always. But right now she was with Alan; they were sharing their own moment. And this feeling that she was having, this wonderful, wonderful feeling, was something that could never be taken away from her.

This knowledge was like an emotional transfusion. It steadied her. Without knowing it she became more graceful than she'd ever been before, and her responses were beautifully instinctive.

This did something to Alan. All at once this was no longer merely a dance but something very special between the two of them. He held her, and they moved into a world entirely their own, Alan leading, Tiffany following. He became more innovative than he'd ever been before, and her response to him was total, so that they were literally, beauty in motion.

Gradually the other dancers faded to the sidelines. Even the orchestra was captivated, so that the lovely strains of the music continued much longer than they ordinarily would have, with Tiffany and Alan moving through the swirling play of the lights, the colors anointing them.

When, finally, the music ended, the silence was total. And then the applause began, and it was thunderous, the dancers who ringed the floor the most enthusiastic of all. Even the orchestra stood to give them an ovation, and as she looked up at Alan's face Tiffany didn't know which of them was the more bewildered by what had happened.

They withdrew, the applause still ringing in their ears, and made their way back to the table quickly, Tiffany wondering how Hank and Camilla had reacted to the performance she and Alan had unintentionally put on.

Hank was not even trying to mask his surprise. His eyebrows were raised quizzically, and he looked at Tiffany as if he weren't sure he could believe what he'd just seen. The orchestra had started playing again. To Tiffany's relief, Hank turned to Camilla and said, "I think it's my turn."

She laughed. "I doubt that anyone here could follow that act," she said, and her admiration seemed sincere.

"I don't intend to try," Hank retorted with a grin. "I just want to dance with you."

They left the table, and, alone with Alan, Tiffany was actually afraid to look at him. She felt so suffused by emotion that she didn't see how she could keep it from showing.

His voice was very gentle. "I'm not sure I know what happened to us," he confessed. "Do you?"

She shook her head. "No."

"You were . . . superb."

She couldn't keep her eyes away from his face any longer. "It wasn't me," she said sincerely. "It was you. You were . . . magnificent."

"Only because I was inspired," he said softly. "I started to dance with you, and it became an . . . an almost spiritual experience, Tiff," he told her. "I felt as if we were alone in another dimension."

"So did I."

"It was a very powerful feeling," he continued slowly. "It was as if something else entirely outside myself took over. Or maybe it was something so deep within myself that I hadn't even known it was there. Did you feel that too?"

She hesitated, knowing that they were getting into very deep water. But then she said, "Yes," the word emerging as little more than a whisper.

"Tiff, it certainly wasn't my intention to go out there and become involved in a . . . well, in a spectacle," he said.

She believed him. "I know that," she told him.

"I hope so," he said heavily. "I wanted to dance with you, it was as simple as that. Just to dance with you, to say a few words to you. I saw you tonight. In the grand ballroom, that is. I hadn't expected you to come to hear me speak, and I was very much . . . moved to think that you'd do so. I wanted to reach you afterward, but there was such a mob."

"I know."

"I'd planned to call you in the morning," he said. "We have to talk, Tiff. It's no good going on this way."

Tiffany was too shaken emotionally to deal with what she was hearing. There was a significance to what he was saying that thundered behind the words themselves, and she wasn't ready to cope with it. And there was something she had to know, though she hated to pose the question to him.

"Alan," she asked him, "just what is Camilla to you?"

"She's a very good friend," Alan said. "We were in medical school together, as a matter of fact. Later she went to Texas to do her residency. More recently she has been on the staff of a large hospital in Hartford, Connecticut. She's a pediatric cardiologist, a very good one. She's also very much interested in the future of transplants. She may be here in Boston herself, within the next couple of years. It depends on her husband, to some extent. He's an obstetrician, and he's built up quite a practice in Hartford."

Her husband. Tiffany was astonished at the intensity of the relief to be derived from just these two simple words.

Their dance over, Camilla and Hank were approaching the table. Alan stood, again holding Camilla's chair for her. Sitting down, Hank said, "I've been trying to persuade Camilla to stay over so that I can put her on my show. Maybe you could help, Tiffany. She's pointed out to me that I had an all-male panel the other night. I get this dismal feeling that she thinks I've neglected the role of women in medicine."

"Oh, come on, Hank," Camilla laughed. "Women have established themselves in medicine; we no longer need a build-up. Anyway, although it would be great fun to be on your show, I have to get back to Hartford tomorrow. After a whole week away I'm going to have an overwhelming number of things to straighten out before I go back to the hospital Monday."

"Are you heading back to Maine tomorrow yourself, Dr. Winslow?" Hank asked innocently, and Tiffany that Alan was staying on in Boston.

"No," Alan said slowly. "I won't be going back to Bangor until next Tuesday morning."

"They've asked Alan to join the staff at the new

Commonwealth Hospital," Camilla said. "A really fantastic opportunity."

"Are you taking the Commonwealth post, doctor?" Hank asked Alan.

"I haven't made up my mind yet," Alan admitted reluctantly.

"Alan, that's the most ridiculous thing I've ever heard," Camilla put in. "Anyone in your field would bend over backward for a chance to get on at Commonwealth . . . especially on the ground floor, which is exactly what you'd be doing."

Alan said carefully, "It would mean moving to Boston."

"And what's so bad about that?" Camilla asked, surprised.

"Who knows?" Alan evaded. The music had started up again. He turned to Camilla. "Dance?" he suggested.

"I can't follow Tiffany's act," she warned him.

"There's no need to try to," he assured her, and they moved off together, leaving Tiffany to wonder exactly what he'd meant by that.

Hank insisted that it would be impolite for them to leave while Alan and Camilla were on the dance floor, and so Tiffany willed herself to sit quietly until they came back, meanwhile refusing Hank's suggestion that they have a third round of drinks.

Once Alan and Camilla had returned, though, Tiffany took the first opportunity to stand up and say, "I'm going to have to call it a night. I'm so glad to have met you, Camilla."

Camilla nodded politely. Hank, teasing, said, "Sure you won't change your mind about staying over and coming on my show, Dr. Vegas?"

"I admit I'm tempted, but there's no way I can stay away from Hartford any longer," Camilla told him with a smile. "Maybe some other time."

"Just give me a call," Hank told her.

Alan was standing. He shook hands with Hank, his face inscrutable, and then turned to Tiffany. "I'll call you in the morning," he told her.

She didn't answer. She felt close to the screaming point; these encounters with Alan were becoming increasingly difficult for her. She murmured her good nights, glad to get out of the Atlantic Room and out of the hotel.

Hank had actually found a nearby parking space, and they walked over to it, Tiffany prepared to sidestep any issue Hank might try to get into tonight.

He said very little though on the drive across town to her apartment. Only when he'd pulled up in front of the entrance did he turn to her to say, "Tiffany, I'm not trying to interfere, but—"

"Hank," she interrupted, "I'm tired."

"Okay," Hank said. "I won't press the point. Not tonight."

Tiffany was content to leave it at that.

Fifteen minutes after she got into her apartment, however, the phone rang.

She answered, certain that it was Hank, about to continue the conversation. Hank never was one to let issues remain unresolved if he could possibly help it.

To her surprise, it was Alan who spoke to her.

"I knew you couldn't possibly be asleep this soon," he said.

"No," she agreed.

"May I come over?" he asked without further preamble.

Tiffany was startled, this question completely unexpected. "No," she said.

"Tiffany, I can't wait until tomorrow, as I thought I could," Alan admitted. "I need to talk to you now. I didn't intend to bring up the matter of my possible appointment to the staff at Commonwealth until—well, until we'd gotten through a couple of other subjects first. But as Camilla indicated, this is a pretty important step I'm facing. . . ."

"A career milestone, Alan?" she interrupted, not bothering to hide her cynicism.

"I was thinking in terms of a personal milestone," he told her after a very brief pause. "If I were dealing with my career alone, there would be no difficulty to the decision. But as it is . . ."

"Yes?"

"It would mean my moving to Boston," he said again.

It was easy enough to know what he was driving at. "Are you suggesting that Boston isn't big enough for both of us, Alan?" she asked him.

"I wouldn't put it quite that way," he said carefully. Then, impatiently, he added, "Tiff, this isn't something we should talk about over the phone. I need to see you, I need to discuss this with you. It involves both of us."

"I don't think so," she countered.

"I know so. Look, if you're afraid I won't be able to keep my hands off you if I come to your apartment, I'll meet you somewhere else."

"Alan," she pointed out, "it's nearly one o'clock in the morning."

"I know what time it is, Tiff. But—hell, there must be some all-night coffee shops around."

"I'm not about to choose one for a rendezvous," she told him.

"Then let me come there. For God's sake, Tiff, we're adults. I think we both know that there are things between us that must be faced, talked out. . . ."

"No," she said, the protest an involuntary one, coming from deep inside her.

"How can you say no?" he asked her. "Hasn't this week proved that neither of us can go on until we resolve what's between us. Hasn't it proved that neither of us has been a whole person for over eight years? We owe it to ourselves, if not to each other, to face up to this, Tiff, and to set the record straight for once and for all."

Everything within Tiffany protested this. She could not trust herself to go into past history with Alan, she could not trust herself to try to resolve anything. It was only over these past few days that she'd learned to how great an extent she'd been deluding herself. She had believed, sincerely believed, that she'd become a "new person." Now she knew that the Tiffany Richards she presented to the world was a sham.

She had worked so hard to build a new image. And since she'd come to Boston to work at the Commonwealth Carlton, she'd had a certain confidence in that image. It was a confidence that had crumpled quickly since Alan's reappearance in her life.

Carefully she said, "I don't want to dredge up the past, Alan. I think you know that."

"Is it that you don't want to, or that you're afraid to?" he challenged, coming much too close to the truth. For Tiffany was afraid, desperately afraid, of what was happening to her.

She'd faced up to the fact that she loved Alan. There

was simply no denying it, certainly not to herself. But loving him, and letting herself become more involved with him were two entirely different things.

Tiffany couldn't handle the thought of letting Alan or any other man really come into her life on a deep level again. Not, she told herself wryly, that there was apt ever to be a man for her other than Alan. But no matter how much she loved him, she shied away from making a real commitment. Marriage, for instance, was something she couldn't even contemplate, in part because marriage could mean having another child. And the thought of suffering as she had when Chad died was more than she could even bear to think about.

Wearily she said, "Alan, it's very late, and I'm also very tired. I really don't think this is the time to get into . . . deep emotional issues."

After a moment he said gently, "You're right, Tiff. At least I'll agree to that if you'll promise to meet me tomorrow."

"I can't promise that," she told him.

"Tiff," he said patiently, "I'm willing to go at your pace; I've already told you I have no wish to rush you. But at least let me talk to you. I've *got* to talk to you!"

Deceit had never been easy for Tiffany. She was inherently honest; even as a child it had been difficult for her to fib about even the simplest things. But now she found herself saying, "It isn't that I refuse to talk to you, Alan. I won't be here tomorrow, that's all."

And this, she decided suddenly, was going to be true. She made up her mind that she'd get out of the apartment the first thing in the morning, before Alan had the chance to check up on her. She'd get out of Boston, for that matter.

She was too tired to make any decisions about where

she was going to go for the day. There would be time
enough to choose a locale once she'd taken her car out
of the garage in the morning. And for that matter, it
really didn't make much difference where she went.
The main thing was to put a little breathing space—a
little thinking space—between herself and Alan.

Chapter Ten

By seven o'clock the next morning Tiffany was driving out of Boston. Although she was tired—she'd not slept well—there was still an excitement to taking off like this.

She'd decided to trek down to Cape Cod, although there was a raw edge to the air, and by midmorning clouds had moved in, erasing the last vestige of sunshine. But by then Tiffany had driven out the Cape to Orleans, and had turned toward Nauset, the first of the great Atlantic beaches. She'd been there last on a summer afternoon when cars had been parked in the big lot bumper to bumper. Now the lot was almost deserted, and she was able to park just back of the beach snack shop, not yet open.

She'd brought with her a heavy, hooded sweat shirt that she put on over the sweater she was wearing. Then she started out across the pale beige sand, her eyes turned toward the sea that stretched before her. The water was a dark charcoal today, and there was a powerful swell to the undulating waves. Tiffany stood for a long time at the top of a low sand dune, watching the waves crest and then break into cascading foam, and she was stirred, as always, by this superb example of nature's force. There was a mystique to the sea that had always enthralled her.

She slowly walked down to the tide line, where the sand was smooth, and then started along the water's edge, moving briskly because she was getting chilly, even with the sweat shirt on.

There was so much to think about. But primarily she felt deeply that Alan should make the move to Boston. From everything she'd heard, this definitely was the right next step for him to take, professionally, and she didn't want to be guilty of blocking it for him. She was already developing too many guilt feelings in connection with Alan.

Despite her conviction that Alan should take the job on the staff at Commonwealth General, though, Tiffany knew that she had to consider seriously the fact that Boston really wasn't big enough to hold both of them. No place would be. Even if they were living in the largest city in the world, there would always be the danger of suddenly bumping into Alan on a street corner. . . .

Tiffany bent to pick up a shell, rubbing her fingers over its smooth surface as she contemplated this thought.

Suppose she did bump into him? Are you that much of a coward, Tiffany Richards? she asked herself.

And the answer came: Yes. I am. It was an answer spoken in a very small voice, but an honest voice. Where Alan was concerned, she was a coward.

She sighed and kept on walking until she finally reached a jutting point of sand. Then she reversed her direction and started the return trek, soon to realize that she'd been walking with the wind to her back. Now she was facing it, and the going was considerably more difficult. By the time she reached the parking lot she was tired and cold.

She stopped at a small restaurant in town for coffee and a sandwich. Then she debated as to whether to continue on out to Provincetown and perhaps linger there at the tip of the Cape for awhile, or to go back to Boston.

She opted to return to Boston. But she didn't want to go back to her apartment, not yet. So, on the spur of the moment, she stopped at a bakery and bought a strawberry cheese cake and drove over to Marlborough Street with it.

Trudy was working on a piece of crewel embroidery with one eye, as she put it, while watching an old TV movie with the other. She was delighted to see Tiffany, and at once put on the kettle so that they could brew a pot of tea.

While they were waiting for the water to boil, Trudy announced, "I'm coming back to work Monday."

Tiffany eyed her narrowly. "The devil you are," she said flatly. "I absolutely insist that you take at least one more week off. Matter of fact, why don't you go down to the Cape and lounge around in a motel there for a few days. The rates are cheaper this time of year, and you could do with a little salt air and sunshine."

She'd already told Trudy that she'd driven to the Cape herself that day. Trudy looked at her speculatively, then said, "I'm not trying to escape, Tiffany."

"Do you think I am?"

"Matter of fact, yes," Tiffany's secretary told her. "But if I remember correctly, you told me your ex-husband isn't leaving town till Tuesday morning. You can't very well hide out till then, can you? Unless you want to move in here with me, of course. But, knowing you, even if you did that you couldn't possibly stay away from the office, come Monday morning."

Tiffany flushed. "Am I so transparent?" she demanded.

"Not transparent, exactly," Trudy said affectionately. "I know you pretty well, that's all. You're very conscientious when it comes to your job; that's why you're so good at it. But even if it weren't for the job, I don't think you could resist going back to the hotel when you know that Alan Winslow will still be there."

The kettle was whistling. Trudy warmed the teapot with some of the water, poured this out, put several tea bags into the pot, added the steaming water and, covering the pot with an old fashioned "cozy," set it aside to steep.

Then she said, "No answer to that, Tiffany?"

"You're implying that I actually want to see Alan again," Tiffany said slowly.

"Well," Trudy asked directly, "don't you?"

"Trudy, why do you think I got up at dawn and drove the better part of a hundred miles down to the Cape?"

"Because you wanted to escape," Trudy conceded. "How would you have felt if he'd found out you were going to the Cape and had come after you?"

It was impossible not to imagine this. Tiffany could

envision herself there at Nauset Beach, turning to walk back to the parking lot only to see Alan coming toward her, tall, broad shouldered, his dark hair ruffled by the breeze blowing in from the sea. And she knew that she would have gone to meet him, she would have *run* to meet him. She would have run straight into his arms.

Thinking about it, she could almost feel the strength of those arms as they encircled her. She could smell the aftershave he used. And she wanted his mouth upon hers, she wanted . . .

She shuddered, and Trudy said, unexpectedly, "There are some things we owe ourselves, Tiffany."

She shook herself out of a disturbing reverie. "What?" she asked.

"If you love him, you're a damned fool to let him go away from you again," Trudy said simply.

Without even thinking about it, Tiffany said, "He never went away from me in the first place."

The words echoed through the little kitchenette. And for the first time Tiffany listened to what they were really saying.

Alan had never left her, she'd left him. She'd never thought about it in quite that way before, but now . . .

She shook her head. "It's too late, Trudy," she said.

"I wonder," Trudy answered reflectively.

"Trudy, we've lived through eight years without each other. We've gone in two entirely different directions."

"But now," Trudy suggested, "perhaps you've reached a crossroads."

"No," Tiffany said, shaking her head. "The analogy doesn't work. Alan's made his own life. Oh, he's been shaken by meeting me again, I don't deny that. It's done pretty weird things to both of us. But . . . that's all there is to it."

"You're sure of that?"

"Yes. There's no doubt about it," Tiffany added flatly, trying to force herself to believe this.

Trudy poured out their tea, and Tiffany cut two slices of the cheesecake. But the day was catching up with her, she realized, as she sat at the little wooden table with Trudy nibbling at the succulent cake. The week was catching up with her, for that matter. She felt totally exhausted.

The tea and cake finished, she said, "I think I'll run along, Trudy."

"I'd suggest a long soak in a gloriously scented bubble bath and then bed," Trudy told her.

"I'll follow your advice," Tiffany promised. "Now you follow mine. No way are you to come in Monday morning, is that understood?"

Trudy groaned. "Tiffany, I'll go crazy with boredom. I'm tired of reading, I'm tired of watching TV and I was never any good at things like crewel anyway. It isn't as if I'd have to overexert myself. Anyway," she finished with an impish grin, "I'd like to see this doctor of yours for myself."

The garage Tiffany used was a two-block walk from her apartment house. Sometimes she let the doorman handle garaging the car for her, just as she sometimes called in advance when she wanted it brought around to the door. But today she decided to leave the car and walk the short distance herself.

She'd not bothered to touch up her makeup at Trudy's. So she felt wind-blown and somewhat grimy and was looking forward to the bubble bath Trudy had recommended.

She nodded to the doorman and entered the shaded lobby of the big apartment building, making her way across the thickly carpeted floor to the self-service elevators. Both of the elevators were in use at the moment, and Tiffany stood watching the indicators, showing that one was at the ninth floor and heading up, while the other was at the twelfth floor and heading down.

When the down elevator arrived, empty, at the lobby level, Tiffany stepped inside and pushed the button for her floor, and the elevator doors began to close. Then she saw a male hand thrust them open, and in another instant Alan was standing beside her.

There was no time to say anything, no time to cry out, even if she'd wanted to. The elevator doors had slid closed, smoothly, and the car was starting its ascent.

Alan looked down at her and said lazily, "Well. This is getting to be a habit."

She stared at him dumbly, and he elaborated gently: "Meeting in elevators."

She found her voice. "And this time is supposed to be strictly by accident too?"

"No," he said, and laughed. "This time is strictly by design."

Tiffany shook her head. "It isn't funny, Alan."

"I couldn't agree more," he assured her evenly. "I've been waiting around for—" he glanced at his watch "—for approximately nine hours."

"And the doorman didn't say anything to you?"

"I told him that I was a physician, and that one of my patients was returning from a trip, and I was to meet her here," he said. "I told him I had no way of knowing exactly when she'd arrive, but it was imperative that I be here when she did."

"And you named this patient?" Tiffany asked suspiciously.

"I'd already produced identification," Alan said smugly. "He didn't ask me to name the patient, though I would have been perfectly willing to do so."

"Me, I suppose?"

"You suppose correctly."

They had come to her floor; the elevator doors slid open. Tiffany made no move to step forward. She said, "Alan, we're going back down again. Then I'm coming up alone. Is that understood?"

"No," he said, and she saw that he was pushing the "hold" button so that the door would remain open. "We're both getting off at this stop, Tiff, and you're inviting me into your apartment. Is that understood?"

"Very definitely not," she said, tilting her chin to a defiant angle.

"I suppose," he said, "that it might be possible to stay here all day like this. Maybe at some point someone will be dispatched to see whether or not the elevator's stuck on the sixteenth floor. But that should be quite awhile from now, and we can handle it when it happens. Meantime . . ."

She glared at him. "I suppose you know that you're being ridiculous," she told him tautly.

"I don't think so," he said evenly. "It seems to me it was ridiculous of you to run off this morning, just so you wouldn't have to face me. Childish, anyway."

"Don't you think," she asked icily, "that the trouble I took to try and avoid you proves that I really didn't want to see you?"

"Not necessarily," he told her, with a poise she envied. He seemed so totally unruffled, while she felt as if minor earthquakes were sending tremors through her entire system.

Alan smiled, a disarmingly wry smile. "Tiff," he said, "I don't want to be heavy-handed about this, but you're not giving me much choice. If you insist, we'll stay here in this elevator until someone really does come to check the situation out. And then maybe we'll both be embarrassed. Though to tell you the truth, I don't much care about that. I've been waiting for eight years to talk to you. Not consciously, perhaps. That is to say, I didn't wake up every morning to tell myself, 'It's four years and six months now that I've been waiting to talk to Tiffany.' Or, 'It's seven years and five months,' or whatever. It was in my subconscious . . . as are a hell of a lot of the most important things that affect us. But it surfaced. It surfaced fast."

Tiffany drew in a deep breath and then faced him, knowing that mere defiance wasn't going to get her out of this. But she wasn't about to comply with his wishes, either. All along she'd been telling herself that she wasn't up to facing Alan, to coping with the emotional struggle certain to follow if they delved into the past together. Well, that still held true. But, dismaying though it was, he was stronger than she was, and she knew there was no way she could force her way out of the elevator and then get into her own apartment and lock the door behind her before he followed her.

The ludicrous aspects of the situation suddenly hit her. She could imagine the headlines in tomorrow morning's *Globe*. "Noted surgeon holds hotel publicity director hostage in luxury condominium elevator." She could imagine Hank Carella's face as he read the story, to say nothing of Trudy's, to say nothing of Grafton Emery's—and the list lengthened.

Reasonably she said, "This isn't the time, Alan. I'll admit I took off early this morning and drove down to the Cape to get away from you."

"Thanks a lot," he said wryly.

"It wasn't quite the way it sounds," she amended. "I needed to get out of Boston; I needed to breathe some fresh air, to think. I drove way out on the Cape and walked along a beautiful, deserted beach, and I tried to reason things out. . . ."

He was watching her closely, his finger still pressed on the elevator hold button. "And did you succeed?" he asked her.

"No," she said honestly. "I think meeting each other as we did has . . . has been difficult for both of us," she continued. "But trying to force issues isn't going to make matters any easier."

"I'm not trying to force any issues, Tiff," he said reasonably. "I want to talk to you, that's all."

"As I've said, this isn't the time," she repeated. "I'm tired, and—"

"You were tired last night," he interrupted. "Early this morning, to be more correct. It was nearly one when I called you. If you left for the Cape at the crack of dawn, relatively speaking, you couldn't have gotten much sleep."

"I didn't," she admitted.

"All right," Alan said. Briefly Tiffany thought that he was going to take his finger off the hold button and let her go. But this was a futile hope.

"Would it be too much to ask you to invite me in for a drink?" he suggested unexpectedly. "Suppose we pretend it's a continuation of our lunch date the other day. Suppose we pretend that you asked me over, and—"

"Alan," she interrupted, striving to be patient about this. "We aren't children. Games are great in their place, but I think we're past the point of playing any more of them."

"I don't agree," he insisted stubbornly. "I enjoyed lunch the other day. I enjoyed it very much. Didn't you?"

"Yes," she said, her patience beginning to fray. "I did enjoy it very much. But that has nothing to do with . . . this."

"I think it does," he contradicted. "Look, it's after four. And it's Saturday afternoon. The combination adds up to a good time for two people to have a drink together, doesn't it? Two people who've just met, but would like to get to know each other a little bit better. Is that so dangerous, Tiff?"

It was very dangerous, and she knew it. Still, the thought of resuming the charade with him, again playing the game they'd played at lunch the other day, had a definite appeal. She'd discovered things about Alan while they were game playing, new facets of this person she'd come to call "the new Alan" to herself. And there was still more to discover, she knew that.

She smiled and said, "All right. You win, Dr. Winslow. I had a great time at lunch with you the other day. I wonder if you might have time to stop by for a drink?"

He gazed at his watch with mock solemnity. "Just one drink," he said. "I do have a dinner date at seven, and I'll have to get back to the hotel and change first."

"I have a dinner date myself," Tiffany lied. "So that will be fine."

Alan let her precede him out of the elevator. Then, finally, he took his finger off the hold button, left the car himself, and followed her down the hall.

The apartment had an eastern exposure, looking out directly on Boston Harbor, a view with a never-ending fascination for Tiffany because it was forever changing. In late afternoon, though, the living room was shadowed. Now Tiffany turned on table lamps, conscious of the man who still stood just inside the front door. He was watching her, she knew, but she suspected that he was also assessing the apartment, and she was sure that he would find it revealing in a way he could not possibly expect. This was her home now, and it showed an aspect of her life about which he knew absolutely nothing.

He said slowly, "That's right. You mentioned that you'd lived in New Mexico for a time, didn't you?"

Tiffany could not instantly remember whether or not this subject had arisen while they were having lunch the other day. But she said, "Yes."

"Were you working out there?"

She couldn't remember whether or not they'd gotten into this either. So she said, "Not in the beginning. I'd had a year and a half of college; at that point in my life I decided to go back to school. So I got my degree at the University of New Mexico. Then I got a job in public relations at a large hotel in Albuquerque."

"And," he said, with a smile, "your career was launched?"

"I suppose you might say so."

Alan had moved across to the window; he was looking out at the harbor. "Terrific view," he said.

"Anything connected with the water always has a fascination for me."

"For me, too," she admitted.

"I should imagine you could spend hours looking out at this," he said, waving toward the view beyond her windows. "Constantly changing. A lot of boat traffic. I wouldn't mind living here myself."

She was determined not to attach any significance to such remarks, so she merely said, "I was lucky to get the place."

"You bought it?"

"No," she said. "I lease it from the owners. I have a long-term lease, and if they decide to sell—they still haven't made up their minds about that—I have first option to buy."

"Quite a gem," Alan said, turning away from the window to face her.

He was in semi-silhouette, the late afternoon shadows sculpting his body so that he was a chiarascuro study as she looked across at him. And it was as if a tangible force emanated from him, stretching out toward Tiffany so that she could feel the strength of its magnetism. She reacted by actually stepping backward.

Again she realized how he had matured in these eight years. Those silver hairs at his temple were only one indication. In other ways it seemed as if his body had become stronger, more emphatic—the shoulders broader, the waistline more tapered, the thighs long and solid. She could imagine how they would feel pressed against her own legs, and an insidious warmth began to creep over her, starting at a very central, core point and shocking her with its intensity.

She'd never before experienced anything exactly like this. Not even with Alan, over those months when they'd been married. There was no negating the physical impact they'd had on each other then, but this was different—and, she knew instinctively, a far more deadly thing to reckon with. Alan had said that they were both adults. She'd not explored the full meaning of that statement. But his mere physical presence was having an astonishing effect on her.

Action, she thought. I've got to do something, I've got to move, I've got to keep busy.

"That drink," she suggested, hoping that her voice wouldn't reveal her own inner shakiness. "What can I get you?"

"What would you recommend?" he asked.

Long ago his favorite cocktail had been a Rob Roy. But she was not about to suggest this to him now. She was not about to let the past invade, because the present in itself was proving to be all—if not more— than she could handle.

"I thought I'd go for a vodka martini myself," she said. He'd never liked vodka particularly, she knew, and she wondered what he might say. But he merely shrugged.

"Make it two," he told her. "Or would you like me to be bartender?"

"Thanks, no, that'll be fine," she assured him, and moved out to the kitchenette, quickly busying herself with glasses, ice cubes and liquor bottles.

He spoke to her from the doorway. "Would you mind if I freshen up a bit?" he asked.

"No," she said, and added, "The bathroom's through the bedroom, to the right."

"Be right back," he told her, and suddenly this struck her. She really was here in her apartment with

Alan. This wasn't a pretend date, this wasn't the second time she'd met with an attractive man who'd come to the hotel to a meeting. This was Alan . . . and all the implications of what that meant swept over her.

I've got to get through this, she told herself, measuring vodka out and pouring it over the ice cubes, then adding a liberal splash of vermouth. I've got to keep on with the game; I've got to convince myself that I never saw him in my life before last Tuesday morning, when he came into my office to speak about publicity for his meetings. I've got to keep up the farce until he gets out of here, and the sooner that is the better, for both of us!

Even now he was in her bathroom. And she knew very well that, en route, he'd look over her bedroom thoroughly.

What would he expect to find? A photograph of himself, perhaps? Or one of Chad? She had no photographs at all here in Boston, no old ones, at any rate. Those few pictures that she'd decided to keep had been placed in a heavy cardboard box and tied up with twine. Her parents had taken the box along with them when they moved to Florida, at her request. She'd wanted no reminders of the past.

She put the two drinks on a small tray and took it back into the living room. Now it was her turn to go to the window and look out over the harbor. One indication of spring was that the days were growing longer. It would be awhile until sunset. Then the lowering rays would send out long, exploring fingers that would reach all the way toward the East, gilding the edges of this scene.

She did not hear Alan come back into the room. And so she was completely unprepared when he encircled her with his arms and pulled her back toward him until she was close against him, her head nestling against his chin.

He said, his voice husky, "How lovely and how lonely you looked, standing there like that." Then he added, "My Tiffany."

Slowly he swung her around to face him, and it was as if everything that had been pent up inside Tiffany was released in a sudden, molten flow. He tilted a finger under her chin so that she was forced to look up at him, and she saw the question in his clear, gray eyes and knew there was only one honest answer to it.

She was committed to him. She was committed both to him and to the moment, and she knew that if she never lived past today she would have lived fully—once she knew the glory of being with him in the entirely new way of which she knew them both to be capable.

His mouth descended, and her own mouth was ready. She felt his kiss even before their lips joined.

Tiffany was rocked by frissons of desire. Her body curved toward him, pressing urgently against him. Somehow her sweater was discarded, and then her wispy, lacy bra. And then he was drawing her jeans down over her slim, tapering hips, his hands following as they caressed every smooth inch of her.

She was not even conscious of moving with him toward the couch. She knew only that all motion was a part of what was happening to her—to them—and that this rapture that she'd never known before was part of the basic source of life itself.

He caressed her first with his fingers and then with his mouth, his tongue trailing flames of quicksilver as it moved, its scorching warmth blazing a path all over her body, until she was breathing so rapidly that he held off, all at once, smiling down at her as he teased, "Take it easy."

"Take it easy?" she challenged back, daring now to let her hands wander on their own voyage of exploration until they had covered him, coming to rest in the most intimate places, reveling in the maleness of him, in the effect she was having upon him, caressing and massaging until he groaned aloud, and in another minute said, "Oh, my God, Tiff. I can't wait much longer."

Neither could she. She parted her thighs and was ready for him as he entered her, gasping from the combination of pain and pleasure that he brought to her as he gave himself to her. It had been a long, long while since she'd been possessed by a man at all, and briefly, just briefly, it was almost like being a virgin again.

But there was nothing virginal about the transcendent moments that followed. She moved with him, ascending, spiraling, traversing galaxies in which the stars and the planets grew steadily brighter until finally there was an ultimate shattering of a thousand colors . . . and they fused in a union so overwhelming that Tiffany began to sob softly, exhausted from both the beauty and the bliss of it.

Alan's breath was coming raggedly. Then slowly its tempo began to subside. He stretched alongside her, holding her within the circle of his arms, while she pillowed her head on his shoulder. After a time she fell asleep, and he lay very still, not wanting to disturb her. Finally he could hold off no longer from the demands of the desire stirring once more in his body.

Slowly, gently, he began to make love to her again, teasing her to wakefulness. And this time was even sweeter than the last, passion staking its claim slowly but so totally that when finally it crested they were on the far, far side of the horizon, dwelling in the closest thing to Utopia to be found on earth.

Chapter Eleven

*T*iffany awakened slowly. The apartment was in darkness. She stretched, then swung her legs over the edge of the couch, disoriented at first and more than a little bewildered.

The silence was total. She was alone. Alan had left. Dazed, she wondered for a moment if he'd ever really been there at all. Then memory came back with a force that made her cheeks burn.

He'd been there. No doubt of that. They'd made love, not once but twice, and she'd been transported into a realm of feeling the existence of which she'd never even been aware.

How could he have left her? She got to her feet, the sense of loss so devastating that she wanted to cry aloud.

He'd left, and he'd turned out all the lights in the apartment before doing so. In order to let her sleep, this out of kindness? she wondered. Or because he'd thought that she'd be less likely to waken if it were dark, and he wanted to make his escape without arousing her. She remembered that he'd said he had a dinner date. She'd responded—purely defensively— that she had one too.

She got up and switched on lamps. Golden light suffused the room, and Tiffany searched her apartment, looking for a message from Alan. She found a scrap of a note, written on a piece of torn paper, in the kitchen.

"Didn't want to wake you," she read. "I'll be in touch later."

For the moment this would have to suffice.

Wearily she went into the bathroom and turned on the hot-water faucet in the tub, splashed in a liberal amount of bubble bath, then watched it foam. She sank gratefully into the tub, tired all over. She tried to remember all she'd ever read about eliminating intrusive thoughts from one's mind.

That didn't work too well. By the time she'd brewed a cup of tea and made a tuna fish sandwich, she knew that it would be impossible to simply sit in the apartment alone for the balance of the evening.

Right now she didn't want to turn to Trudy, or to Hank, or to anyone else she knew. She remembered that there was a foreign film she'd been wanting to see at a cinema complex in Brookline. She checked the paper to find that there was still time to make the late show, if she called a cab. This she did, and fortunately the film was highly entertaining. It was in French, and Tiffany tried not to rely on the subtitles in English but to test her knowledge of the language, which she'd studied both in high school and college. Even without words, though, it was a funny picture, with excellent pantomime. For a couple of hours she sat munching on the chocolate peppermints she'd bought in the theater lobby and very nearly managed to forget about Alan.

Alan had left the apartment shortly before seven o'clock. Tiffany was sleeping soundly, her face a pale blur in the darkness. He had stared down at her longingly as he gently disentangled his right arm, which had been holding her lightly. He'd loved her for almost as long as he could remember, or so it seemed to him, but he didn't think he'd ever before loved her quite as much as he did now.

He was scheduled to meet Camilla Vegas and two of the other doctors who'd been attending the meeting for cocktails in the hotel at seven thirty. Then they were all going over to Cambridge, to a Greek restaurant that had been recommended to them.

Straightening after easing himself off the couch, Alan wished that there was a way to get out of the dinner engagement. But he knew that Camilla and the others had been doing the sight-seeing bit all afternoon. They'd planned to walk the Freedom Trail, which highlighted some of Boston's historic landmarks. To place a call now—in the hope that at least one of the group would already have returned to the hotel—would be to wake Tiffany, and the doctor in him made him want to let her sleep. She'd been looking exhausted lately, though fatigue had not in the least diminished her beauty. And he knew he was at least partly responsible for the shadows beneath her beautiful dark eyes. This week had been as hard on her as on him; he had no illusions about that. And it had been very hard indeed on him.

He settled for scrawling a brief note to her, then left the apartment quietly. Downstairs the doorman called a cab for him, and within minutes he was back at the Commonwealth Carlton. He showered quickly, shaved with the hasty precision he'd learned, of necessity, while an intern, and then switched suits and put on a fresh tie. These gestures were all automatic, and his mind was racing as he made them.

He was well aware that nothing had been resolved between Tiffany and himself that afternoon. They had only proved that the intense physical attraction between them was greater than it had ever been.

They'd yielded to their mutual desire, but their passion had been inspired not by sexual hunger alone, but by the deep love which, he was now convinced, they still shared.

This was the one thing of which he had been uncertain. After the kiss on the stairway the other afternoon, he'd known where they stood as far as the physical aspect of their relationship was concerned. And he did not underestimate the importance of this powerful feeling. But at first he'd not equated it with love—not the kind of love he wanted from Tiffany, anyway.

For eight years he'd lived with the knowledge of the tremendous mental and emotional barrier between them. And this, he knew, was something that still had to be surmounted. But he had a lot more faith in their mutual ability to surmount it now than he'd had when he'd entered Tiffany's apartment that afternoon. She would not have yielded to him as she had, she would not have given herself to him so gloriously, if she did not love him. He knew her too well to think otherwise.

Alan had spoken to Dr. Anthony Donato twice on the telephone now, and he was to meet him at the

Commonwealth Medical Center on Monday at eleven A.M. They would have lunch together after he'd gone through the hospital and been thoroughly briefed on the position that would be his, should he decide to make the move from Maine to Massachusetts.

He would be expected to give Tony Donato his answer over lunch; he knew that. But even now he was not at all certain what it would be. It depended so much—he corrected himself—it depended entirely on Tiffany. Within the next thirty-six hours, give or take a few, he was going to have to manage to be alone with Tiffany in an environment where they could, finally, face each other and talk things out.

How to arrange that?

At the moment Alan had no idea at all.

Sunday had become a special day to Tiffany, because over the years she'd made it so. It was her day, a day to recoup from the stresses of the week and to indulge in little luxuries that were seldom, if ever, a part of a usual workday.

She was determined that this particular day in April would be like any other Sunday, though she knew that it would take more effort than it usually did to make it so. She got up early, dressed in jeans and a bulky sweater and went for a brisk walk, crossing through the Quincy Market area to a bakery that specialized in all sorts of homemade pastries.

Today she chose flaky croissants. With these, she retraced her steps back to her apartment house and then brewed a pot of espresso coffee before changing into a flowing pink natural silk caftan, with matching scuffs. Then she heated milk and made a fragrant cup of café au lait by pouring the hot milk and the hot coffee into a big china mug. Just the right amount of sugar was stirred into this. Next Tiffany fixed a tray with her coffee, the croissants, and a generous cube of sweet butter, and took this into the living room, placing it on the coffee table with the Sunday paper.

The croissants were as delicious as ever, and so was the coffee, but she found herself skipping over items in the paper that she would usually read carefully. Sunday morning provided her with the opportunity to catch up with the week's news in depth. But this morning she was too restless to concentrate even upon Hank's column, which she usually enjoyed thoroughly. Hank was original and witty and unerringly chose subjects that had a wide appeal and were also capable of sparking controversy. Tiffany was sure that it was her own fault, not Hank's, that today's column fell flat.

She'd opened the wide living-room windows, and the soft air swept across the room, bringing with it more than a hint of spring. It was unusually warm for April in New England, and Tiffany found herself wishing that she had someone to play tennis with. Normally she would have asked Trudy, but that was out of the question in view of Trudy's recent operation. Grafton would have been a likely candidate under other circumstances, and she knew he'd be only too willing to drive her out to the exclusive club of which he was a member. But matters between Grafton and herself were on the shaky side, just now. And certainly the last thing in the world she wanted to do was give him any hint of encouragement.

No, today she'd have to go it alone. She thought of wandering over to the Aquarium later in the day, or perhaps taking a ferry out to one of the harbor islands and exploring. Yet, that sort of enterprise almost demanded a companion. It simply wasn't the sort of thing that was fun to do alone.

Even as she was thinking this, the phone rang.

Alan said, "I tried to reach you a couple of times last night, then I decided it was too late to call again. I was afraid you'd have come home in the meantime and gone to sleep." He paused. "Good morning," he said then. "And it is a good morning."

"Yes, it is," Tiffany agreed, and wished that there were some way for a person to prevent her pulse from skipping about so erratically.

"Any special plans for the day?" he asked. And before she could answer, he added, "I've asked the garage to bring my car around. Let's go drive somewhere, shall we? Sort of a short auto cruise to nowhere?"

"I'm sorry," Tiffany said quickly, "but I can't."

"You do have plans, then?"

Plans. Tiffany said carefully, "Sunday is sort of . . . my own day, Alan. My catch-up day."

"Don't you ever make any exceptions?"

"I try not to."

"Look," he said, "it's much too nice to stay indoors. You owe it to yourself to get out."

"I've already been out," she told him. "I went over to the bakery to get some croissants and took the long way around just because it was so lovely."

"Croissants, eh?" he mused. "Sounds delicious."

"They were delicious," she agreed, wondering if this was a bid on his part to be invited to breakfast. "Past tense. Not so much as a crumb left."

"Glutton," he accused.

"On Sunday morning, yes," she said.

"You buy yourself croissants every Sunday morning?"

"Sometimes brioche, sometimes cheese or prune danish," she said. "It varies. But I do pamper myself on Sundays, yes."

He laughed. "I've never thought of you as a sybarite, Tiff," he admitted. "Though I guess indulging one's appetite once a week isn't all that much of a luxury. So . . . what else do you do on Sunday?"

"Catch up, as I said," she told him. "Correspondence, beauty routine . . ."

"Come on," he protested. "You don't need any beauty routines."

"Ah, but I do," she insisted. "For instance, after a while I plan to put on my mud mask."

"Your what?"

"My mud mask. It's a special sort of mud, green clay, really. It comes from a region of France where they've been digging up mud to make women beautiful for centuries."

"You're putting me on!" he accused.

"No, it's the truth."

"Regardless, Tiff." He was serious now. "I need to talk to you today. I need to see you. Yesterday . . ."

Tiffany, remembering yesterday, experienced a sudden surge of feeling that was treacherous in its impact. It was as if there were electrical wires running throughout her body, and now they'd been stimulated to a quivering intensity. The feeling was so acute that she actually shivered.

Yesterday. Memory washed over her, and with it came a desperate yearning.

It would be so easy, so easy, to give in to him. To do anything he wanted her to do.

She forced herself to say carefully, "Yesterday happened, whether it should have or not."

"What's that supposed to mean?" he demanded.

"I blame neither of us for it, Alan."

"*Blame?* How can you speak of blame? You felt the same way I did, Tiff; you know damned well you did."

"Yes," she admitted, "I did. I'm not denying the . . . the physical attraction we obviously have for each other. Yesterday we both got carried away by it. But that doesn't mean we should let it happen again. We were . . . physically attracted . . . from the first time we met each other. And I think we found out that it wasn't enough. Not enough then, not enough now."

"Oh, for God's sake," he began, a ragged edge to his voice, but then he paused, and she knew that he was getting control of himself. Alan was good at getting control of himself. When he spoke again, it was emotionlessly.

"I know that physical attraction isn't 'enough,' as you put it," he told her. "But yesterday there was much more between us than desire alone. I wanted you; I wanted you more than I've ever wanted a woman before in my life. Even you. But when we came together, Tiff, you know damned well that there was something so . . . so special . . . that . . ."

Her pulse was pounding. And it was hard to keep her voice steady as she said, "I don't want to go into it, Alan."

"I'll have to ask you to go into it," he insisted stubbornly. "I mentioned, I'm sure, that I've been asked to join the staff at the new Commonwealth

Medical Center. It's a great honor, a tremendous opportunity. But the problem is that I have to make my decision by tomorrow. I'm to meet the doctor who has offered me the post at the hospital. He's going to take me on a tour through the whole facility. Then, at lunch, I'm to give him my answer."

Alan in Boston. Though she'd already done her share of thinking about this possibility, the idea that it might actually happen was completely unnerving. Still, she managed to say, "I don't see what that has to do with me."

"Then you're blind," he told her bluntly. "It has everything to do with you."

"You're wrong about that, Alan," she said. "It's your career, your decision, I have no part in it."

"You know that's not so," he accused, bitterness creeping into his voice as he added, "You know very damned well that's not so. Imagine . . . if I were here in Boston and we kept running into each other. I don't know how many more encounters I could take like the one in the elevator the other afternoon."

"The element of surprise would be gone," she pointed out. "And if we wished to, I think we could manage to avoid each other."

"Do you wish to avoid me, Tiffany?" he asked her.

What could she say to this?

"Look," he continued, "it's ridiculous to try to talk about something like this over the phone. And I know what you're saying. Or perhaps I should say I know what you're not saying. This past week has been as difficult for me as it has been for you. I don't want to repeat it any more than you do. But I also realize that we can't make believe forever that we've just met and have started dating. That was fun for an hour or two, but there's been too much between us, Tiff. We can't suppress it forever. We . . ."

He was getting on dangerous ground. She said tensely, "Alan, I really don't want to go into this."

To her amazement he said, "I think you owe it to me."

"What?" The single query fully conveyed her astonishment.

"Exactly," he told her grimly. "Eight years ago you walked out on me. You've never given me the chance to explain anything about—anything. I think I deserve that chance."

Tiffany stared at the sunlight invading her room and found herself blinking away tears. She said, "It's too late, Alan."

"Is it? Well, maybe you think so; maybe you're right. But I'm not convinced, Tiff. Eight years ago you were a very pretty girl. But a girl. Now you're a very beautiful woman, but despite the facade you've built for yourself, I've still glimpsed that girl at moments. I think you still have times when you're lonely and frightened, and I like to think that there have even been times when you've wondered if you should have let me talk to you after all. Am I right about that?"

She could not answer this at once. Then honesty compelled her to say, in little more than a whisper, "Perhaps."

"Tiff, I'll make a bargain with you," Alan decided. "If you'll come out for a drive with me, I promise not to get into the past. Not today. I'll start with where we are right now and take it forward. But I want you to hear about this job offer; I want you to evaluate what I have to say to you and then give me your opinion about the course of action you think I should take."

"That's putting too much responsibility on my shoulders, Alan," she protested. "I have no right at all to say anything about your possible course of action, especially when it involves something that will seriously affect your career."

She let it go at that, but he got the message. This became clear when he said wryly, "And my career matters to me more than anything in the world, right?"

"I should think so, yes," she said, trying to keep this low-keyed because, again, they were approaching dangerous ground.

"I won't go into that," he said abruptly. "Not on the phone, certainly. Can you be ready in half an hour?"

"I don't intend to be ready at all," she reminded him.

"Then I'll come sit in the hall outside your apartment until you either have me thrown out bodily or let me in. If you won't go out and have lunch or dinner with me somewhere and let me talk to you, I'll bide my time until you meet me on your home ground."

"Not again," she said swiftly.

"That's what I thought you'd say. Okay, then. Thirty minutes?"

Tiffany hung up without an answer.

She was angry, thoroughly angry. And she discovered, to her surprise, that this was the first time she'd ever been truly angry with Alan. Resentful, yes. Hurt, yes. In fact, she could list a whole gamut of negative emotions she'd felt about him eight years ago. But anger, burning anger? No. This was something new. And strangely it actually seemed healthy.

She seethed as she went into her bedroom, where she

pulled out her new Katharine Hepburn–style white cotton pants and teamed them with a sweater banded in broad stripes of pink and white. She tied a pink bandanna around her throat with a flourish, then chose some comfortable espadrilles. She was in the mood for walking. She might very well walk all over town today. Or maybe she'd take a bus somewhere out of town and walk there, she decided defiantly. She wasn't in the mood to drive.

At the last moment she threw an oversize pink sweat shirt over her arm, just in case it was cooler out than she thought it was—or should become so before she returned home. Again she felt the need to escape. To escape Alan, to be precise about it. But combined with this was a stirring that she couldn't remember ever experiencing before, a nomadic sort of feeling. She could imagine herself a gypsy, about to start off on a fantastic adventure. She wanted to roam!

She dug out of her closet a braided Italian straw bag that she'd not used since last summer—it seemed just right now. Into it she thrust her makeup case, a small folder with all her charge cards in it, her wallet, which contained a fair quantity of cash, sunglasses, a paperback novel she'd been reading—just in case she wanted to find a deserted park bench somewhere and curl up in the sun and read—and a roll of cinnamon candies she'd bought at the hotel newstand the day before. Plus a comb. She hesitated. Did she need anything else?

She laughed at herself. She was acting as if she were really about to embark on a safari . . . but in a sense she was. She would not be coming back here until Alan had given up on his game of standing guard outside her apartment. For though it seemed a ridiculously childish gesture for a man of his stature, she was sure that this was exactly what he was going to do.

Going down in the elevator, she thought about Alan. Elevators, she was very much afraid, were always going to remind her of Alan!

Why, she pondered, was he so insistent about talking over his job opportunity in Boston with her? True, she couldn't imagine Boston, or anyplace else, being big enough to hold both of them; she'd already reached that conclusion. But if it came down to basics, it seemed ridiculous that they couldn't cope with this situation on a purely adult level.

The elevator doors opened at the first floor, and Tiffany breathed an involuntary sigh. She'd almost been afraid that she'd find Alan outside her apartment door, although there had not been time for him to get across the city unless he had a magic carpet.

Now, she half expected him to be waiting for her on the ground floor, but he wasn't. And she experienced a mixture of relief . . . and disappointment.

Relief dominated. As she crossed the lobby she told herself that this sort of thing wasn't Alan's style—wasn't his style at all. Alan was much too dignified to camp on someone's doorstep. At least the Alan she'd known had been, and surely Alan, the surgeon, was even more distinguished and sophisticated; he would be beyond playing such childish games.

She considered this and realized that she wasn't all that sure about the "new" Alan. She was quite intrigued with him and wished that she could get to know him without danger. But yesterday had precluded that. Yesterday, the "new" Alan and the "old" Alan had merged in a combination that was utterly devastating.

Tiffany told herself that she could not risk such an assault upon herself again. He was right when he'd said it hadn't been the physical union only that had been so important. No, there had been more than that. And she was afraid, terribly afraid, of where it all could lead.

She reached the entrance doors and stepped out onto the street. The sunlight was brighter than she'd expected, and she paused to open her bag and grope for her sunglasses.

She'd just found the case and was about to open it and slip on the dark glasses, when she felt her elbow being gripped and looked up into Alan's smiling face.

"There you are," he said amiably. "I was just telling Terence that maybe I'd better run upstairs to see if you'd fallen asleep again. Those antibiotics do tend to make one drowsy."

He was acting the part of a physician, she realized as he gripped her arm more firmly and led her toward the curb. She glanced back at Terence—the doorman—to see him smiling at them benevolently. Clearly Alan was no villain in his eyes but rather a doctor come to minister to the sick. A doctor who, in this day and age, was even willing to make a Sunday house call.

Tiffany gritted her teeth as she felt herself being propelled along and knew that to try to escape would only result in a scene.

"Let me go, damn you!" she hissed. "How did you get here so quickly?"

"I called you from the corner pharmacy," Alan hissed back, then added in a pleasantly audible voice, "A ride out of town and some dinner in a country inn will do wonders for you, my dear."

And with that, he thrust her into the front seat of the silver-gray Saab at the curbside, managing to do this so that any passerby would actually have thought he was being very courteous.

"Don't try to get out," he cautioned in a low voice as he closed the door after her. "You may not know it, but I'm a pretty damned good runner. For all of your prowess at tennis and jazz ballet and the rest, I could catch you before you got to the corner. And I would have absolutely no hesitation about using a flying tackle if necessary."

She believed him. She retreated into silence, aghast at all of this, and as she glanced across at his profile while he inserted the key in the ignition and started the car, she wondered if the eminent Dr. Alan Winslow had actually taken leave of his senses.

Was she in the hands of a psychotic? A madman, who would stop at nothing to get his own way? These concepts were so utterly ludicrous in connection with Alan that she dismissed them as quickly as they occurred to her. And yet there was something almost menacing about this handsome, dark-haired man dressed in jeans and a thick white sweater who was driving the Saab out into a stream of Sunday traffic on the Southeast Expressway as if he were accustomed to highjacking women every day of his life.

As they neared the turnoff to the Callahan Tunnel and Logan Airport, she even wondered for a moment if he might be thinking of spiriting her aboard an airplane and flying off with her to—to where?

But this thought passed as they continued north over the Mystic River Bridge.

Only then did she decide that it was ridiculous to sulk

in silence. And so coldly she asked, "Where are you taking me?"

He took his attention away from the traffic long enough to grin down at her.

"For a mystery ride, shall we say?" he suggested.

And Tiffany had to be content with that.

Chapter Twelve

$\mathcal{T}$iffany lapsed into silence. If Alan was back in a game-playing mood, she wanted no part of it.

On the other hand, she didn't know what to do next, what to say to him. She was tempted to be both dramatic and daring and to jump out when he was next forced to slow down. She might suffer a few bruises, but she was reasonably agile. As long as she didn't leap right into the path of a car, she should be able to avoid real injury. And it would create quite a scene. In fact, it would serve Alan right, she decided.

His voice cut across her thoughts.

"I'm glad you find something amusing about this," he told her.

"I don't," she returned quickly.

"Well, you were smiling," he observed mildly.

This had been at the thought of the revenge she would get should she have the courage to try this form of escape. Or rather, should she be foolhardy enough to attempt it, she amended. The traffic was heavy. If one of the drivers suddenly saw a girl jump out of a moving car, there was no telling what might happen.

"Tiff," Alan said suddenly, "I'm sorry I had to resort to theatrics. All I wanted was to talk to you. But I found myself up against a stone wall, and I knew there was no way you were going to come around. My next chance would have been to try to pin you down—excuse the expression—in your office tomorrow morning. And that would have been too late."

"Too late for you," she said bitterly, and added, knowing that she was being unfair, "You've always thought of yourself and your career first, Alan."

She was surprised at his reaction. He didn't so much as glance toward her, but it was as if his profile, studiously directed toward the road, had turned to stone. His face was granite hard, and his gray eyes were glacial. Tiffany flinched, instinctively moving closer to the door.

After a moment he said quietly, "I'll ignore that. I intend to have time to make my points with you, Tiffany. And when that time comes, we can get into the matter of my career . . . and your misconceptions about it. But this isn't the moment."

He continued, reasonably, "Look, I'll strike a bargain with you. Give me the next few hours of your time, voluntarily. Listen to what I have to say. Let me hear your viewpoint. Not about the past, Tiff, I agree. I don't think we should get into the past until we've solved the present."

"You're talking in riddles, Alan," she accused.

He shook his head slowly. "No, I'm not. You and I are living now. Not yesterday. We can't undo yesterday. There's nothing quite so final, so irreversible, as the past. Eventually, I know, we may have to come to terms with it, but that will depend upon what we decide to do today."

"There's nothing for us to 'decide to do today,'" she mocked. "Please take the next exit off this highway, will you, and reverse directions?"

"No," he said flatly. "I will not."

"Sooner or later you're going to have to stop, Alan," she told him. "Whenever it is, wherever it is, I'm going to get out of this car and get away from you. Do you realize that I could have you arrested for kidnapping?"

She was looking directly at him as she said this, and immediately wished she hadn't. Because his smile was enough to twist anyone's heart. It was the epitome of sadness.

Ruefully he said, "You make me out to be a monster, Tiff. But then I've been a monster in your book for a long time, haven't I?"

"I'm not even going to dignify that with an answer," she told him. "You have to admit, though, that this whole escapade is . . . insane."

The traffic was heavy at this point, and he didn't answer immediately. Then he said slowly, "Yes, I suppose it is. I don't blame you if you think I've flipped. I admit I was desperate. Desperate to talk to you, that is, nothing more. But . . . yes, this is crazy."

She was surprised at his ready agreement, and not entirely sure she believed in it. But nodding, she said, "All right, then. Let's turn around and go back to Boston."

"May I make a suggestion?" he countered.

"I don't think so," Tiffany said, at once wary.

"Tiff, we'll be in Portsmouth shortly, and all I'm

going to suggest is that we stop there for lunch. Are you familiar with Portsmouth?"

"New Hampshire?"

"Yes. New Hampshire."

"No. I'm not."

"It's an old town," Alan said. "Settled in the early seventeenth century, if I remember correctly. A long, long time ago it was the capital of the state of New Hampshire, and home port for some of the wealthiest seamen in New England. They built some magnificent homes. The town is full of wonderful examples of both Colonial and Federal architecture. You'd love to do a tour of it."

He was right about that. Tiffany had always been interested in early American architecture; once they'd spoken of either buying a very old house and doing it over or else building a new one that was a faithful reproduction. But now she responded only by saying, "Not today, thanks."

"I'm not suggesting today," Alan said patiently. "You might want to come back sometime, though, and spend a couple of days here. The town's engaged in a restoration project called 'Strawberry Banke,' and they're doing terrific work. They've got thirty-five different buildings in various stages of restoration, down in the historic waterfront district. You can take a walking tour, rather like the Freedom Trail in Boston."

"Alan, look," she said, "I don't mean to be nasty, but spare me the travelogue. I'm not in the mood for it."

"I wouldn't expect you to be," he agreed. "Nevertheless, there are some good restaurants around Portsmouth, and frankly, that's what I'm interested in at the moment. I thought you might enjoy going to an old farmhouse that dates back to the 1840s and has been converted into a popular eating place. They make great chowder."

She sighed. "I'm not hungry," she told him.

"That's right," he said, "you had those special croissants for breakfast, didn't you?"

She glanced across at him suspiciously. He was smiling again, but this time there was humor in his smile, and despite a surface annoyance at him, she was inwardly relieved. She wasn't sure she could bear to see that intensely melancholy look on Alan's face again.

"Breakfast was a long time ago," she reminded him.

"Ah, then maybe you could go for some chowder. And home-baked strawberry-rhubarb pie," he suggested.

Inexplicably her mood lightened, and she very nearly smiled herself. "All right," she conceded. "You're making me hungry."

"Good," he applauded.

They fell silent, and after a time Tiffany realized that she was studying his hands as they gripped the steering wheel. Long ago she'd noted that they were a surgeon's hands. Beautifully sculpted, with long, capable fingers. They were firm hands; they could also be amazingly tender. She shivered slightly, remembering the way he'd caressed her the day before, those hands covering every inch of her during the course of their provocatively sensuous explorations.

They came to a traffic circle. Alan negotiated it skillfully, then turned into a side road. At the restaurant he'd chosen they found the parking lot so full of cars they doubted they'd be able to get a table. But as it turned out, there was room for two more. They ordered chowder and strawberry-rhubarb pie, both of which were as good as Alan had promised they'd be. As if by unspoken consent, they said very little as they ate, merely enjoying the excellent food. But Tiffany began to feel as if she'd been warmed internally, and this had nothing to do with the steaming hot chowder. She couldn't quite believe in it, but a definite rapport seemed to have arisen between Alan and herself. She was experiencing an easy sense of camaraderie with him; she felt comfortable, right.

The dessert finished, he flashed her a smile. "Was it worth it?" he asked.

It was impossible to answer him immediately, because the smile had taken its usual emotional toll on her. But then she swallowed hard and managed a hasty "Yes. I really did enjoy it."

"Good."

She followed him out to the parking lot, and it was not until she was seated in the front seat of his car again that she remembered her threat to escape from him the first time he stopped anywhere. Strange how something could change so suddenly. Just now she had no desire to escape from him at all. She felt lazy, contented, full of good food, and the April sunshine slanting through the car window was an added benediction.

Alan put the key in the ignition switch, but he didn't immediately turn it. Then, to her surprise, he said, "I wish the boats were running out to the Isles of Shoals."

"What?" Tiffany demanded.

"You've heard of them?"

"I don't believe so."

"They're a group of shoal islands a few miles off the coast," he told her. "They straddle the Maine–New Hampshire boundary. I went sailing out in that area a couple of times last summer. Once we ran into fog, and it was an eerie experience. Most of the islands are very bleak, uninhabited. But there's a conference center on one of them—Star Island. We put in there until the fog lifted. There's a sprawling white-framed house—I understand sometimes writers try to book space out there to get away from it all. And one really would get away from it all. . . ."

"Is that what you have in mind?" she asked him, the caution flag beginning to flutter again.

"No. In the summer, though, you can take a boat on a tour out through the islands that lasts a couple of hours. I've never done it, but I want to sometime. There's a lot of history involved. For instance, on one of the islands—Smuttynose—there was a famous, extremely macabre murder back in the last century. I've read about it, and—"

"You want to visit the scene of the crime?" she asked incredulously.

"Not exactly. I suppose it's simply that I've come to love the seacoast, and everything it has to offer. All the history, the legend. The days of the mooncussers, pirates . . ."

She shook her head. "You surprise me."

He laughed and finally did turn the ignition key; the motor purred into action. But then, as he started the car, he said, "Would you do me a very big favor?"

That feeling of easy camaraderie vanished as quickly as it had arrived. "What?" she asked suspiciously.

"Tiff, don't look at me like that! It's just that there's something I'd like to show you, that's all. Something very important to me."

"What, exactly?" she asked him. "And where?"

"Just a piece up the road," he told her, grinning

lazily. "Seriously. It would only add a couple of hours to our trip; you could still be back in Boston before dark." Those compelling gray eyes met her dark ones, and held them. "Please," he said simply. "It would mean a great deal to me."

Tiffany stirred uncomfortably. "Must you be so mysterious?" she asked him.

"In this instance, yes," he told her. "Humor me, will you, just this once."

He could be beguiling, very beguiling. Tiffany was thoroughly aware of this. On the other hand, she rationalized, it was a beautiful day, and she'd not gotten out of the city like this for a long time. The drive to the North Shore with Hank for dinner the other night wasn't in this category.

"All right," she said reluctantly, and Alan flashed her a surprisingly boyish smile.

"That's terrific," he said enthusiastically.

She noticed that he was heading back to the traffic circle, but instead of veering in Boston's direction she soon realized that he was going north, and almost immediately they were driving across a high bridge.

Tiffany stared down at the wide river far beneath them as Alan said, "The Piscataqua. It divides New Hampshire and Maine."

"Maine?" she echoed, shocked. "Look, Alan . . ."

"Maine isn't the end of the world, Tiff," he reminded her gently, "and I'm not about to take you to the deep woods. We'll stay strictly along the seacoast, okay?"

"It might be okay if you'd tell me just what it is you have in mind," she pointed out.

"I want to surprise you."

"I'm not at all sure I want to be surprised," she said

tautly. "In fact, I don't think I do. Look, Alan, we've played enough games, wouldn't you say?"

"I agree," he said seriously. And added, "I promise you, Tiff. This will be the last one."

Again he was concentrating on the highway, his face inscrutable. Tiffany stared across at him, hating the unavoidable feeling of helplessness that came over her. But she had no one but herself to blame for this, she reminded herself. She'd been an idiot not to break away from him in Portsmouth and find her own transportation back to Boston.

As they drove on Alan didn't seem to be any more inclined to talk than she was. When finally he switched off Route 1 and onto a road that became narrower and narrower, she began to be really apprehensive.

"Look," she said, close to real anger, "just where are we going?"

"You'll see in a few more minutes," he told her. And, true, he shortly switched off onto a lane that ended at a rocky beach, where an old pier jutted out into the water.

It was a deserted place. Perhaps in summer it might not be so, Tiffany conceded, but at this time of the year the loneliness of the landscape struck her. The rockbound coast of Maine. She'd read about it, she'd seen pictures of it and now she experienced it, but despite its beauty, she wished herself far away.

Alan said cheerfully, "Okay. Get out. This is the end of the line. The temporary end of the line, anyway."

She stared at him. "What are you talking about?"

He waved toward the water lapping at the pebbled shore. "We're on an inlet from Muscongus Bay," he said laconically.

"That means absolutely nothing to me, Alan."

"No, I suppose it wouldn't." To her astonishment, she saw that he was walking toward the old pier, and then she saw the boat tied up at the shore end of it. It was a wooden boat with an outboard motor propped up in the stern.

Alan said, "Tide's low. So at least you won't have to get your feet wet."

"What?" The question was an outraged one.

"Come along, Tiff," Alan said agreeably.

"You *are* out of your mind!" she accused, actually backing away from him.

"Maybe I am," he agreed lightly. "We'll soon find out. Look, Tiff, I'll carry you over and put you in the boat, if you prefer."

"I don't prefer anything," she said icily. "I have no intention of getting into that boat with you."

She was still close to the car. Now she backed herself up against it, a sudden thought forming. In a swift motion, she ran around the front and got into the driver's seat, quickly locking it behind her. She was so sure she'd find the key still in the ignition switch that she reached her hand out from force of habit, not even looking. And her fingers closed around empty space.

Alan had followed her. Now, to her chagrin, he simply opened the door on the side of the car where she'd been sitting and slid in next to her.

Tiffany flinched from the expression in his eyes. They were cold, metallic. "So," he said, "you really would have run off and left me here if you'd had the chance, wouldn't you?"

"Yes," she assured him defiantly. "Yes, I would!"

"There might not be anyone along for hours, maybe even a couple of days. Maybe even longer," he said.

"There aren't many people around here this time of the year, and this is private land."

Private land. Did that mean there was a house nearby?

He seemed to read her mind. "There used to be an old farmhouse up over the rise," he told her, "but it burned down a couple of years ago."

Was he merely saying this to keep her from exploring, or was it true?

Tiffany sighed, a deep, shuddering sigh. This whole thing was unbelievable! It couldn't be happening to her . . . with Alan Winslow, of all people. Despite anything she'd ever thought of him, she would have relied on the fact that he was one of the most civilized, self-possessed, level-headed persons she'd ever met.

What, in God's name, had happened to him?

He said calmly, "Look, we can sit here until hell freezes over, for all I care. I have a lot of patience, Tiff. But it would make more sense if we got going now."

She shook her head miserably. "I don't know what you're talking about! Going where?"

"You'll see," he told her mysteriously.

"Alan, I thought we'd agreed that we've played enough games. May I remind you that you promised to get me back to Boston before dark?"

"I remember that, yes," he evaded.

"We've come a long way since Portsmouth," she told him. "All right. The Maine coast is magnificent, I'll agree to that. Some other time I'd like to come back and see more of it. But right now, I want to go home. So, please . . ."

She was trying to reason with him and knew she'd been too obvious about it when he said, "I'm not a child, Tiffany. Nor am I an idiot. I asked you to come along with me because there's something I want to show you. That still holds. And that's all there is to it. So if you'll just follow along and get in the boat . . ."

Tiffany gazed back longingly at the rutted road down which they'd driven the last stage of the way and tried to calculate how far it was back to the better road, and from there to the first road onto which he'd turned off Route 1.

Almost gently Alan said, "It would be a long hike, Tiff. And frankly, unless you've changed a great deal, I'll have to remind you that you've never had the greatest sense of direction."

He was remembering Lake George, she knew, when a couple of times she'd gotten hopelessly lost. And there had been other occasions, when they'd had the chance to go off for picnics and such during the early months of their marriage.

"Come along," he said. Then she saw a spasm of pain cross his face, and he added, huskily, "Do you really think I'd do anything to hurt you, Tiff?"

Tiffany was so confused at this point that she couldn't respond with a ready negative to his question. The moment when she could have assured him that she did know—deep in her heart—that he would never deliberately hurt her passed, and his mouth tightened.

He reached across her and flicked up the lock on the door. "Don't bother pushing it down again," he advised her then. Next, he got out of the car, came around to her side and flung the door open, staring down at her.

"I guess I'll have to carry you," he decided.

Tiffany stiffened. "Thank you, but that won't be necessary," she assured him, and moved out of the car and on toward the boat, her head held high.

Alan helped her into the boat, and then got in easily, stepping down from the edge of the pier. He swung the motor downward, and started it with a couple of quick tugs of a cord.

"I came down just before I went to Boston and got her into the water," he explained. "I took her for a trial run out into the harbor then, so she's ready to go."

Go where? Tiffany wondered apprehensively.

"I didn't know I'd be having such a lovely companion on my next trip out," Alan went on, steering the boat expertly as he spoke.

There was a breeze out on the water. After a moment Tiffany slipped on her sweat shirt and zipped it up, and Alan said, approvingly, "I'm glad you brought that along."

She glanced at Alan. He was concentrating on what he was doing, but she was suddenly aware of a tenseness about him, and this only served to alarm her further.

Finally he pointed ahead and shouted, above the noise of the motor, "That's where we're heading."

Tiffany, gazing out toward the direction in which he was pointing, saw absolutely nothing at first. Then she became aware of a very low shape on the horizon, one of several low shapes.

An island!

Why, in God's name, was he taking her out to some remote, offshore Maine island?

The gap between land and water began to close swiftly. Tiffany saw, then, that the island was larger than she'd thought at first, and certainly not flat at all. In fact, the side toward which they were heading seemed to be sheer rock, topped with spiky green pines.

Then Alan changed course slightly, circling around the rocky ledges that jutted out from the island shore until, rounding a point, he came into a small, protected cove.

He cut the engine, and the boat slowly putted toward a stretch of shore that was sandy at this particular point. Then, in the shallows, he dropped an anchor overboard and said with a grin, "There's no reason why we should both get wet. Stay put, for a moment."

With this, he rolled up his trouser legs. Then, in a surprisingly graceful movement, he went over the edge of the boat, and Tiffany saw that he was standing in water that came only to the middle of his calves.

He held out his arms to her. "Come on," he said.

"No," she told him firmly.

"Tiff, if you don't mind, this water is frigid," he pointed out. "So stop stalling, will you?"

"I don't want to go ashore, Alan."

"First you didn't want to get in the boat, now you don't want to go ashore," he said, shaking his head at her. "Look, Tiff, this isn't the time to be perverse. My teeth are starting to chatter."

"That's your doing," she reminded him.

He frowned. "Very well," he told her. "You can spend the night right where you're sitting."

With this he turned, starting to trudge through the water while she stared disbelieveingly at his retreating back. She couldn't believe that he'd actually leave her to fend for herself in this—this stupid little wooden boat. Yet that was precisely what he was doing, and she had a good idea that he wasn't about to change his mind and come back for her—unless she asked him to.

Her voice was small. "You win," she said disconsolately, and at first thought he hadn't heard her. But then he turned, returned to lift her out of the boat and cradled her in his arms as he covered the distance to shore.

As he set her down he laughed, a laugh edged with bitterness. "Trust a woman!" he commented. "You actually remembered to bring your handbag along with you."

She had. She'd instinctively reached down for the straw bag before he'd lifted her out of the boat; now it dangled from his arm.

"It's just as well," he observed ominously. "You'll probably need it."

She'd already posed too many questions that he hadn't answered, Tiffany decided. She wasn't going to give him the satisfaction of asking another one.

He bent to rub his legs with his palms. "I think my blood froze," he commented, then said, "Okay. Come along."

Tiffany saw that a path began curving at the end of the sandy beach, almost immediately disappearing into the thick pine woods just beyond. Alan was heading for the path, and there was nothing for her to do but follow him.

It was a winding path, uneven and quite rocky in spots. Tiffany made her way along it carefully. The last thing she wanted to do right now was to fall on her face and thus force him to come to her rescue.

The path was also uphill all the way, reasonably steep in spots. But then, around a curve, it both straightened out and leveled out and Tiffany, looking ahead, gasped in surprise.

She was gazing upon a clearing that literally had been hewed out of the woodland on three sides. The third side faced toward the sea. A log cabin stood in the middle of the clearing, situated so that its windows would get full advantage of the water view. But despite this one open side to the weather, the site for the cabin had been designed so cleverly that there was a natural barrier to protect it from the elements.

There was a great deal of charm to the cabin. It reminded Tiffany of pictures she'd seen of pioneer structures, on long-ago frontiers. Yet it had a contemporary look to it too. A wide roof overhang covered the porch that stretched across the front, and in the roof itself a number of skylights had been cut to let the warmth and the sunlight in. A second level rose in back of the roof with the skylights, with a wide, open deck. In summer, Tiffany suspected, there would be lounge chairs out on that deck, and it was impossible not to imagine what a delight it would be to laze out there with a good book and that glorious, glorious expanse of Maine's beautiful water as a "front yard."

Tiffany became aware that Alan was watching her very closely. His smile was crooked as he asked, "Like it?"

"It's absolutely enchanting," she said honestly. "Enchanted, too, I'd say. I can't believe I'm seeing it! Who does it belong to?"

She'd no sooner voiced the question than she knew the answer. He only confirmed it when he said, "Me."

"Yes," he added, "not too long after I moved to Bangor I had the chance to buy the land where the old farmhouse stood, plus this island. This swatch of land had already been cleared. And so," he finished, "I built the log house. There are still a few more things to be done inside, but it's fairly well finished, now. I spend every minute I can here, except in the dead of winter. In summer I keep a sailboat as well as the outboard.

"This place," Alan finished, as if speaking to himself, "could be a paradise. At least it seemed so to me."

He stopped speaking so abruptly that the resulting silence startled Tiffany. He'd been about to say more, she suspected, then had decided against it.

Now, while she watched him, he pushed back a strand of dark hair that had fallen forward over his forehead, and there was a touching weariness to the gesture.

"Come on," he said. "Let's go inside. I'll get a fire going, and I have the makings for drinks."

Chapter Thirteen

·

Tiffany lingered at the bottom of the steps that led up to the wide front porch. Alan had gone ahead of her; now he was waiting for her while again watching her closely.

After a moment he stirred, and she sensed his impatience. He called down, "Well?"

Tiffany started up the steps slowly. Alan had flung open the front door, and he stepped back so he was directly behind her. At once she was overwhelmingly conscious of his presence . . . his presence and his tenseness.

"Go on," he urged.

She stepped into a large room, two sides of which were paneled in pine. But one side was an entire glass wall overlooking the sea, giving the effect of a miraculous merging of sky and the water. Tiffany, mesmerized by it, stared out into incredible blue space and said, "It's fantastic, Alan."

"I hoped you'd say that," he told her, his voice husky. "Now . . . what do you think of the fireplace."

She swung around to view the enormous fireplace opposite the glass wall. A huge stone chimney went straight to the ceiling. There was a raised hearth, and the opening itself looked big enough to burn an entire tree. Large logs had already been set into place. Alan touched a match to the newspapers wedged between them, and Tiffany saw flames edge along the paper. Then slowly the logs began to crackle until soon there was a fire so inviting that she went across to hold out her hands before it, savoring its warmth.

She noticed that there were old-fashioned hurricane lamps placed on most of the tables, some of them with plain glass shades, some of them with more elaborate, hand-painted ones. And there were candles in a variety of interesting holders, some of them brass, some copper, all of them, she suspected, antique.

Curious, she asked, "No electricity?"

"Not yet." Alan shook his head. "One of these days I'll do something about it. For the moment, though, I've been content to rough it. I haven't missed the bright lights . . . any kind of bright lights," he embellished.

"I shouldn't imagine that you would."

"No running water, either," he added. "We have a good well, though. We never lack for water, you just have to work harder to get it, that's all. As for plumbing . . . someday I'll go modern. In the meantime there's an old-fashioned outhouse a short distance through the woods at the rear of the house. Primitive, true. But clean."

Then he added, "I've rigged a system so that I keep a supply of water in a pantry off the kitchen during the months when I come here. It'd freeze during the winter. I stocked up, though, when I came out here a couple of weeks ago. So whenever you want to wash up, you can get all you want in gallon jugs. Relatively portable."

Tiffany was still standing in front of the fire, almost as hypnotized by the flickering flames as she had been a little while earlier by that marvelous panorama of sea and sky. Now she said quietly, "It seems as if you've found a real retreat for yourself."

"Yes," he agreed, and she sensed that he was about to add something more, only to switch abruptly and say, "Now for a drink. Scotch okay?"

"Yes."

"I'm afraid I can't offer you ice." He laughed. "The amenities will come in time," he promised. "For the moment the well water is cold . . . and quite delicious."

"It will be fine," she told him.

She was looking around at the other things in the room. The furniture was either pine or maple, all of it antique, she was sure. The wood had that lovely patina that comes only with age. The tables, the chairs, the big old cobbler's bench that served as a cocktail table in front of the large, comfortable, upholstered couch, were all pieces that had seen a great deal of use over many years and had been given tender, loving care during the course of it.

On the couch there were throw pillows in a range of vivid colors. No curtains at the windows. That, too, would come later, she imagined, and it would be a crime, actually, to cover the glass wall. One would have to be careful with the type of curtain treatment used there.

A rough wooden staircase, fairly narrow, ran up the left wall, toward the rear. Above, there was a landing that served as a balcony overlooking the room. She suspected that there must be two bedrooms off the balcony, judging from the size of it.

"You must wish you could live here," she said softly.

"I do," Alan admitted. "But needless to say, that'll be out of the question for many years to come. In the meantime, as I said, I come here whenever I have any extra time at all. I haven't had as much of that as I'd like either. My schedule would be better—or so Tony Donato promises me—if I move to Boston."

"How far are we from Bangor?" she asked.

"A couple of hours drive," he said absently. "Boston's about the same distance, a little bit farther, actually." He came across to her now, holding two glasses, one of which he handed to her. "I need this," he admitted. "I should have known enough to leave some high rubber boots in the boat. It'll be a while before the water's warm enough around here to go wading."

Tiffany sat down on the couch, her eyes still on the fire, and sipped the Scotch. It was good Scotch; it went down very smoothly. Alan stood with his back to the hearth. His silhouette was outlined in a bronze glow, and he looked very tall, very powerful. She could imagine him working out here on his island, building the house. She asked, "Did you build it alone?"

"What?"

"This," she said, gesturing around her.

"No." He grinned. "I hired two local guys who are excellent carpenters, and I worked with them. I learned more over the course of a couple of summers than I could have from anyone else in several years. They are craftsmen, those two. Painstaking. You'd be amazed at the care with which this place has been put together."

"No," she said, "I'm not amazed. It looks like a place that will . . . endure."

Alan moved away from the hearth and came to sit down on the couch, but not beside her. He chose the far end, as if he were determined to keep as much distance as possible between them, and this surprised her. His face was in the shadows. But hers, she knew, was lit by the firelight, and this made her feel vulnerable. Right now he could see her much more clearly than she could see him.

He said quietly, "Tiff, I know I've gone about everything in entirely the wrong way. But I wanted you to see this place . . . so much. I hadn't intended for it to be so soon, I hope you believe that. In other words, I had absolutely no intention of . . . well, of kidnapping you. I just knew, this morning, that I had to talk things out with you. I thought maybe we could simply go for a drive, somewhere out of Boston, and find a quiet spot. Then . . . well, by the time we got to Portsmouth I'd come to realize that it would be very easy to bring you here . . . even unwillingly."

He shook his head helplessly. "I've botched things," he confessed.

Had he? Tiffany wasn't sure. It was impossible not to be glad to be here with him, even though she knew she should resent his high-handed tactics.

"Tiff," he went on, "as I've told you before, as I told you on the way down here, I don't want to go into the past with you. What I want to talk about is where we are now, and where we can expect to be tomorrow. All week I've driven myself nearly crazy trying to sort things out. Tomorrow I've got to go face Tony Donato, and if I refuse him this time around, he's not going to give me any future offers. But you see, I know . . ."

He drained the rest of his whiskey and set the glass on the coffee table. "The fact of the matter," he said, "is that I know damned well I can't live in Boston if you're going to be there too."

Tiffany bristled. "Are you suggesting that I be the one to leave town?" she demanded.

"No!" he interrupted harshly. And then added more quietly, "I realize you've made a place for yourself in Boston, and I respect your work. I'm proud of what you've done." He got up, pacing across to the hearth again, clearly very much agitated.

"All right," Tiffany said, trying to be calm about this. "All right! I jumped to conclusions. But what else could I think when you said that you know you can't live in Boston if I'm going to be there too?"

She still could not see his face clearly; in fact, the room was growing even more shadowy. But he turned toward her, and he was still as a statue as he asked, ironically, "Might it not occur to you that I reached the conclusion I can't accept the job . . . unless you and I can effect some sort of compromise?" It was impossible to find a quick answer to this, and after a moment Alan said, tautly, "You're very quiet."

"Yes," she admitted.

"I thought that when I used the word *compromise* you'd issue an immediate challenge." He hesitated. "Can I make you another drink?"

To her surprise, she saw that she'd finished her first one. She hesitated. She seldom drank very much: her work demanded a clear head, and she'd never liked the effect of much alcohol anyway. Now she certainly needed to have all of her wits about her. Yet she found herself saying, "Yes, please. But make it mild, will you?"

He did make it mild. She took a sip, then placed the glass on the coffee table and said, "I admit . . . your use of the word *compromise* did come as a surprise to me."

"Can't you imagine that we might be able to compromise . . . on some things at least?" he asked dryly.

"I hadn't thought about it that way."

He strolled back to the couch, sat down again, still keeping distance between them. "The other day when we went out to lunch together I guess I got somewhat carried away by my own game plan," he said. "And to tell you the truth, it wasn't all that hard to pretend that I'd met you only the day before. You've changed a great deal, Tiff."

She laughed shakily and couldn't resist the query, "For better or for worse?"

"In most ways I'd say you've changed for the better. You're even more beautiful than ever, and you've learned how to handle that beauty to maximum advantage. You've learned how to dress and to use makeup to enhance your looks. You've cultivated yourself, Tiffany."

"I don't like the sound of that," she protested.

"I'm not accusing you of having become narcissistic," he said quickly. "It's more as if you've taken clay that was lovely in itself and made something even more lovely out of it. Something unique. I find you a unique person, Tiffany. But . . ."

"Yes?"

"Something's been lost along the way," he said quietly, this startling her. "At least it seems so to me. I suppose I could be trite and say that long since you lost your girlish laughter . . . and God knows you had reason enough to do so. But it's not quite that. It's just that you used to be so warm, so loving, so caring. Now . . . I don't sense that same quality in you, Tiff. Or is it simply that you've learned to camouflage it in self-defense?"

She forced a laugh. "Are you sure you haven't changed your specialty to psychiatry?" she asked him.

"No. Anyway, I'd make a lousy psychiatrist. No," he repeated, "it's just like going to light a lovely candelabra, only to find that one of the candles is missing."

She forced a light touch. "Only one?" she asked him.

"Only one." His next comment surprised her completely. "Do you ever look in the mirror, Tiffany?" he asked her.

She frowned, puzzled. "What's that supposed to mean?"

"It's a rhetorical question, admittedly. But . . . I wonder," he said. "I wonder what you see when you look in the mirror. Did it ever occur to you that our mirror image is reversed?"

She wanted to get away from this sort of thing with him. She laughed. "Alan," she asked him, "is this what you brought me up here for? To philosophize?"

"No. Or maybe I should say, partly. I brought you up here because I wanted you to see the island, I wanted you to see the house."

"And you own all of it?" She could be honest enough about her astonishment over this. She couldn't imagine owning an entire island, even a relatively small one.

"Plus that land on the mainland where you keep your boat?" she added.

"Yes. There are still good buys to be had in Maine."

"Even so." She picked up her drink again and sipped cautiously. It would be so easy to down the whole thing in one swallow, she was so edgy. "Even so," she repeated, "it must have cost a small fortune. I know that doctors are reputed to make a lot of money, but—"

"I didn't buy the island from my medical earnings," he said flatly.

"Oh?"

"You sound surprised. Am I to believe that you really are surprised, Tiff?"

"Why shouldn't I be?" she asked, more surprised than ever at this point.

Again he stood, but this time it was to light one of the hurricane lamps on an end table. It gave the space around it a lovely glow.

"I want to see your face," he said simply, "and it's getting too dark in here. Tiffany, are you telling me that when you married me you didn't know I'd inherited more than a small fortune from my parents?"

She stared up at him. "No," she said dumbly, "I didn't know. We didn't seem to want for money, true. But I never questioned that. I suppose I thought that you had a . . . a scholarship or something." She listened to her own words, and shook her head. They sounded so inane. She'd been so naive. How could anyone ever have been that naive?

"You knew my parents had died when I was ten?" he queried.

"Yes. You told me your uncle had brought you up."

He nodded. "My uncle is Felix Winslow. He's senior

partner in the firm of Winslow, Homer and Atchison . . . which is one of the top law firms in New York. My father headed a large investment firm. But he'd already inherited most of his money before he even became involved in it. It was an old fortune, Tiff, going back, way back, to the days when there were staggering amounts of money to be made in this country and almost no taxes to pay."

He paused. "I was an only child, you knew that?"

"Yes."

"The money was placed in trust for me, according to the terms of my father's will," Alan said. "My education was paid for, and I received a fairly liberal allowance during my school years. But I didn't come into the principal until I was thirty-two. Don't ask me why thirty-two was supposed to be the age of reason, but that's what was determined in this case."

"Why are you telling me this?"

"Why? It might make the compromise I'm about to suggest somewhat more attractive," he said dryly. "I can't offer you the moon, Tiff, but I can surely offer you the next thing to it."

"What are you saying, Alan?"

"I'm asking you to come back to me. I'm asking you to marry me again."

Tiffany felt as if she actually were going to faint.

Alan peered down at her. "Tiff, are you okay?" he asked, after an anxious moment.

Tiffany pressed a shaking hand to her forehead. "I'm not sure," she confessed.

"Hey!" To her consternation he dropped down on his knees in front of her, just avoiding the edge of the coffee table. He reached out to touch her thigh, and he said, "My God, you're trembling!"

Her teeth were chattering as she tried to answer him, so that she stuttered out the words. "I'll be all right in a minute," she said.

He stared at her, his gray eyes pain-filled. He looked as if she'd struck him, and he said, "I didn't expect this sort of reaction. It would seem," his voice shook slightly, "that I've botched it again."

His hand moved away from her thigh: he cupped her chin with those long, slender fingers she loved so much. "Dearest," he said, "for God's sake don't look at me like this. I've gone about everything in all the wrong way because . . . because time's running out. But . . ."

When she remained silent, he muttered something under his breath and in another moment was on his feet again, moving out the coffee table so that he could step behind it. Before Tiffany knew what he was about to do he'd lowered himself to the couch, directly next to her this time, so close that she could feel the warmth of his body. He drew her into his arms, cradling her head against his shoulder, and he said softly, "No, don't start protesting. Don't say anything. Just calm down."

Tiffany fought back laughter, as she knew that right now it could only lead to hysterics. Such proximity with Alan was the one thing guaranteed to keep her from calming down at all.

He said soothingly, "Just take it easy, Tiff. God, you're white as a sheet. Look—"

"I'm all right Alan," she insisted, trying to pull herself away from him. "It was a shock, I admit. I didn't expect—"

"Yes," he interrupted, an odd note in his voice. "I can see it was a shock. Not exactly flattering, but I suppose I have it coming."

He was still holding her with his left arm, but his right arm was free. And now he caressed her hair, separating the pale gold strands and letting them fall between his fingers. She could feel herself responding to his touch, those familiar, electric currents beginning to pulsate through her again. It would not take much, she knew, to toss caution away entirely. Not much at all. Now was the time to free herself from his tender embrace. Now was the time to tell him that he'd already violated his promise to get her back to Boston before dark, but that they must at least leave now so that they could get across the stretch of water to the mainland before it was too late to see anything.

But she didn't move, nor did she say anything. There was something so wonderful about having him hold her like this, gently, so gently. His fingers played over her neck and then moved downward. They found their way beneath the edge of her sweater, and involuntarily she edged toward him, making it easy for him to unfasten her bra. The Scotch, the warmth of the fire, even the glow of the hurricane lamps, were heady influences, acting like aphrodisiacs.

She turned toward him, raising her arms to clasp his head, to make it easier for him to kiss her. A light kiss at first, an incredibly tender kiss, the pressure of their lips gradually increasing until their mouths became hungry with desire, their tongues seeking, probing, finding their own fulfillment.

And this was only the beginning. Slowly Alan drew her down so that she was lying against the inner curve of the couch, and then he was lying next to her, his hand moving over her constantly in an arousing pattern that made her feel as if every cell within her had been dormant until now, when all of them were springing to life at once. Her responses to him heightened, and she saw that his eyes had turned dark, very dark. Involuntarily she began to undulate her body as her own hands started to move, outlining his head, the strong thrust of his throat, touching his shoulders and moving downward until she came to the hardness of him, and then she felt a sweet-sharp surge of triumph because she had the power to arouse him like this.

He moaned, "Oh my God, Tiff!" And the tempo between them increased as they undressed each other until, finally, they were both lying naked, their skin made golden by the firelight. "Dearest, dearest," he groaned, "I can't wait too much longer."

But there was no need for him to wait at all. She was ready for him as he entered her; she matched him as they merged together; she kept pace with him until the entire universe shattered; she was caught in its afterglow, spiraling through space in a dark and wonderful world that was, somehow, showered with silver.

They lay, spent, within the circle of each other's arms. She didn't want to say anything; she didn't want him to say anything. This was their now, a time without past, without future. Tiffany let herself be encapsulated by it and only wished that she could dwell within it forever.

"What can I say?" Alan asked.

"I don't think there's anything for either of us to say," Tiffany agreed tightly.

"Tiff . . . There was . . . nothing wrong about it," he said. "You know that, don't you. Two people couldn't . . ."

She stirred restlessly. "Please," she said. "I don't want to go into it."

They were sitting on the couch in front of the fireplace; it was dark outside. Alan had lighted additional hurricane lamps, and they cast a warm glow through the room, making little golden oases.

Alan had insisted on making scrambled eggs for them and some biscuits, fried in an iron skillet. "Camp-style cooking," he called this, and he was good at it.

He had a cooking stove that used bottled gas. "Fortunately," he said, "I saw to it that there was a supply sent in last time I came over."

This "last time" had been the first time since winter. The first chance he'd had to get away from the hospital, he'd explained. It stood to reason, Tiffany reflected now, that the preparations he'd made then had not included her. He would have had no way of knowing that they were so soon to cross each other's paths once again.

Now he rose to put another log on the fire and to ask, "Tired?"

"Yes," she said, and this was true. She was emotionally exhausted. The day had taken a toll, she felt totally drained by it.

Hesitantly he said, "Only one bedroom is furnished, Tiff. I'd offer it to you, but it wouldn't be very generous of me. It's going to be cold as an old-fashioned icebox. There will be fireplaces in the bedrooms upstairs— eventually there will be two of them—but there's still some masonry work to do. You'd be more comfortable staying down here, on the couch. I'll bring down some pillows and a couple of quilts."

She nodded indifferently. Right now she felt as if she could go to sleep in an old-fashioned icebox. She needed sleep. She needed it desperately . . . as an escape. She needed to get away from Alan. And the only way to do it was to fall asleep, deep asleep.

He had not repeated his astonishing offer again. He had not mentioned marriage. What was it he had asked her to do? To come back to him, that was it. The last thing in the world she'd ever expected was to have Alan Winslow propose to her. Her ex-husband proposing to her! There seemed something vaguely indecent about it.

Alan said, "Your eyelids are drooping." Then he added, "Stay put for a minute."

As if she had anywhere to go. She'd already made her pilgrimage to the outhouse "up the path out back." It was a new experience, but Alan had been right. The primitive facility was meticulously clean. She'd shivered all the way back to the house. Then Alan had poured water into a basin for her, so that she could wash her face and hands. And he'd given her a wry smile, saying, "Sorry, but I don't think there's a toothbrush in the house."

She'd almost teased him about this. She almost said, "Wow! And you a doctor!" Or something of the sort. But there was an intimacy to humor. Better to keep it straight, she decided.

What was it that he'd told her he'd found lacking in her . . . in her new image, that is? Warmth . . . loving . . . caring. She winced a little, thinking about this. He'd implied she'd been brushed by Pygmalion in a reverse sort of way. She'd been converted into a porcelain statute. Lovely, but with no heart.

She heard his footsteps echoing on the wooden stairs. The fire was wonderful. She curled up at the end of the couch, watching the flames. One big log split, sending out a shower of copper sparks. Watching them, Tiffany felt her eyelids become so heavy she could no longer hold them open.

Alan came back down the stairs laden with pillows, two old-fashioned patchwork quilts, and a pair of his own well-worn flannel pajamas.

He found Tiffany asleep, her long lashes brushing against cheeks that seemed very pale, her long, light gold hair framing a face that was etched indelibly in his mind. She looked very young, very vulnerable. Watching her, he sighed, a sigh that came from the depths of him. Then he gently inserted a pillow under her head and drew a quilt up over her.

He settled himself down in a big armchair after pulling closer to the fire and wrapped himself in a quilt, using the other pillow to cushion his head. But he slept lightly. It was the kind of sleep he usually got when he was on call in the hospital. He could come out of it in an instant, fully alert.

There'd be no need for that tonight, he knew. But over the next hours, the fire would go out unless he kept adding a log to it now and then, and he wanted to keep Tiffany warm.

He rephrased that.

He wanted to keep Tiffany.

Chapter Fourteen

*T*iffany awakened the next morning feeling amazingly refreshed. She sat up on the edge of the couch and stretched luxuriously. It was the first time she could remember that she'd slept a sleep devoid of dreams.

To her surprise, she saw that the fire was still blazing. Looking more closely, she realized someone had put another log on not long ago. Alan, of course. Probably it had been so cold upstairs he hadn't been able to sleep comfortably.

She'd thrown her sweat shirt over a chairback last night. She found it, put it on and let herself out the side door, heading toward the woods. She used the primitive facilities, but on the way back to the house she detoured, going across the clearing to the water side, where there was a rocky ledge that jutted out, a natural observation point. The view was as incredible as she'd expected it to be. A sapphire sea, a turquoise sky, other little islands in the distance, all of them with rocky outcroppings topped with the spiky pines. How marvelous it would be to sail among them, to explore.

When she got back to the house, she could smell the delicious aroma of bacon being fried. Alan was at work over the stove again. He'd already poured out her basin of water for her. She splashed her face with it, and then, finding her handbag, combed out her hair and added just a touch of lip gloss to her mouth. The fresh, cool air had brought a rosy glow to her cheeks. She really didn't need makeup this morning.

"Come and get it," Alan said cheerily, and she sat down at the round oak table in the corner of the kitchen, sniffing appreciatively as he set a plate of food in front of her.

"It's the salt air," he said, smiling. "Guaranteed to give a lovely lady a man's appetite."

Alan looked terrific this morning. Evidently he kept clothes on the island, because he was wearing faded jeans and a very becoming heavy-knit gray sweater. He'd shaved, there was a fresh, ruddy look to his cheeks, and he'd combed his hair neatly into place. Tiffany longed to run her fingers through it and muss it up.

He put a plate of bacon and eggs for himself on the table, then pulled out a chair and sat down opposite Tiffany. She watched him butter a biscuit, then spread it thickly with strawberry jam. And an odd little knot caught in her throat. A lump that wouldn't go away, even when she swallowed hard.

There was something very intimate about sharing breakfast with Alan like this. Something very . . . precious. She'd not fully realized until this moment how much she'd missed him, these past eight years. She admitted to herself now that Alan had never left her heart; he was a basic part of her being and always would be.

She was looking at him with that heart in her eyes. And suddenly he glanced up to meet her gaze. She caught the flicker of expression that crossed his face. A bittersweet sadness. And she saw his gray eyes grow cloudy. But then the moment passed, and he smiled at her.

"More coffee?" he asked.

She shook her head. "No, thanks."

She was puzzled by his behavior. He was so friendly this morning. Yes, that's exactly what it was. He was being friendly, considerate, but nothing more than that. There was nothing of the lover about him, or of the man who, only a few hours ago, had pleaded with her to come back to him, to marry him again.

Tiffany could not help but conclude that at some point during the night Alan had changed his mind about a lot of things. Now she sensed none of yesterday's tenseness, anxiety. No, Alan had gotten hold of himself, and at the moment he was in complete control.

He finished his breakfast and took his plate, cup and saucer over to the sink.

"I don't want to hurry you," he called over his shoulder, "but we'll have to get going before long. Otherwise you'll be late for work."

Work was the last thing on her mind. It astonished her to realize that she'd actually forgotten all about the hotel and her job there. The thought of leaving the island so soon . . . She wanted nothing so much as to explore it with Alan. This house, the island . . .

She said, "We can't possibly get back to Boston in time for me to go to work anyway, can we?"

He chuckled. "Indeed we can, if we don't dawdle. Daylight comes early here, Tiff. Maybe you haven't looked at your watch, but it's not quite six thirty. So, if we get going . . ."

She remembered now that he had an appointment himself this morning with a doctor at the new Commonwealth Medical Center. And remembering, she realized what had happened that had so changed Alan's attitude.

He'd made his decision. He'd made up his mind about whether or not to accept the Commonwealth staff position. And having done this, he'd freed himself from worry. He was his own man again. No more tension. No more anxieties.

She grimaced. It was beginning to seem as if she'd inherited those tensions, those anxieties. She didn't think she could keep on breathing unless she found out, quickly, what it was he'd decided. And yet she couldn't bring herself to come out and ask him.

Maybe, she concluded, he'd tell her on the drive back to Boston.

She took her own dishes over to the sink and plunged them into the basin of water Alan had set there.

"I'll do them up," she offered.

"Don't bother," he advised. "I'm coming back on the weekend, and I plan to do a good cleaning job. Anyway, there's no time to heat water."

She turned away, feeling as if she'd been rebuffed, which was ridiculous. But he'd turned down her offer of help so quickly, making clear at the same time that he was capable of handling things by himself.

Alan made sure that the fire was out, then stacked the quilts and the pillows in a neat pile on one end of the couch. After a final look around he said cheerfully,

"Well, I guess that's it," and a moment later they were going down the front steps and starting along the path to the beach.

At the bend in the path, Tiffany could not refrain from turning and looking back at the house snuggled against its protective background of fragrant pines. Overnight she'd fallen in love with the place. Now, she thought sadly, she'd probably never see it again. She had the strong sense that this was going to be the end of the line for Alan and herself. She had an intuitive feeling that the decision he'd made did not involve her. Nor, she was sure, was the suggestion that they remarry ever going to be made to her again.

This time he pulled the boat up on the beach and helped her into it. Then he shoved off, climbing in himself before it got very far and using the oars to push the boat out into deeper water so that he could start the motor.

Tiffany found herself wishing that the motor would fail to start. Or that something, anything, would happen to prevent them from leaving here.

But the motor roared into action, and in a moment they were leaving the island behind them.

She said wistfully, "It's a lovely spot, Alan."

She caught a flash of surprise on his face, but he only nodded agreement.

The trip back to the mainland seemed shorter than the trip out had. Now Tiffany hoped that the car wouldn't start but, to her chagrin, it functioned perfectly. In much too short a time they were driving along the roads that led to Route 1, and from then on the passing miles seemed, to Tiffany, to be creating a new kind of distance between Alan and herself.

He seemed disinclined to talk, although his affable

mood persisted, and Tiffany could find nothing to say to him under the circumstances. They spoke, occasionally, about the weather or some of the scenery along the way, but they could have been two strangers insofar as the content of their conversation was concerned.

As they were nearing Boston he said, "I suppose you'll want to go to your apartment first."

"Yes. I'll need to change," she told him.

"I can wait for you, if you like, and drive you on over to the hotel," he offered.

"Thanks," she said, "but I don't want to hold you up. I can take a cab."

He didn't protest. Rather, Tiffany got the impression that he was just as glad he wasn't going to have to wait for her. This morning Alan seemed eager to get on with his own business.

A dozen times she nearly brought up the subject of Alan's appointment with the doctor at the Medical Center and the decision he would have to give before the day was through. Mentally she phrased and then rephrased questions about this, but no matter how she put it they seemed unduly inquisitive. So when he let her out in front of her apartment house, she was as much in the dark as ever.

He had to double-park; there was no chance to linger. Looking across at him, Tiffany knew that the letdown from this weekend was going to be terrific. She was already beginning to sag mentally.

It was he who spoke first. "I guess this is good-bye," he told her. "I've decided to drive back to Bangor tonight."

This was a shock. She knew that originally he'd not been scheduled to check out of the Commonwealth Carlton until the following morning.

"Alan," she began, "I—"

"There's no need for you to explain anything to me, Tiff," he cut in. "I think I understand, in fact I'm sure I understand. I hope you'll forgive my high-handed actions yesterday, but . . . I'm glad, regardless, that you saw the island."

She found herself answering softly, "So am I."

"Tiff, I've got to move on. There's a taxi trying to get in here."

"Yes." She nodded. She wanted nothing so much as to reach across and kiss him. She felt so impelled just to touch him that she clenched her hands to keep from doing so.

"I hope that everything will be wonderful for you, Alan," she said. Then she slipped out of the car and ran toward the apartment house door without looking back, her eyes brimming with tears.

Tiffany was late for work that morning. Alan had gotten her home in plenty of time, but once inside the apartment she had dissolved. She'd made tracks for her bedroom and flung herself on her bed, and then the tears had come, and she'd cried torrents of them.

After a long time she'd staggered to the bathroom and splashed her face with cold water. Only then had she gone to the phone to call her office, with the intention of reporting that she'd be in later.

To her astonishment it was Trudy Barnes rather than Sally Grant who answered the phone, and Tiffany promptly forgot about her own problems.

"What are you doing there?" she demanded.

Trudy chuckled. "I told you I was coming back to work, boss lady," she reminded Tiffany.

"And I absolutely forbade you to do so," Tiffany

exploded. "Trudy, you get right out of there and take a cab home and—"

"No," said Trudy gently. "Sally's gone back to sales, so there'd be no one to hold the fort if I did that. Anyway, this is therapy for me. I feel better than I have in ages."

"It was exactly a week ago today that you went into the hospital for major emergency surgery," Tiffany said severely. "It's absolutely ridiculous for you to be back at work."

"Even my doctor said it was okay, provided I took things easy and didn't lift anything heavy," Trudy reported. "Now, what about you? Don't tell me *your* appendix has flared up?"

"I had it out when I was twelve," Tiffany said abruptly. "Trudy . . . I'm going to be late."

"You already are late," Trudy reminded her gently.

"All right. I'm going to be later, then. I'll be in as soon as I can pull myself together. Meantime, just don't do anything, do you hear?"

"Very well," Trudy said with mock obedience. "I will fold my hands and just sit here, and if anyone asks me anything I won't answer them."

"That's fine with me," Tiffany said tersely. "Does Grafton know you're back?"

"Yes. He welcomed me into the fold again."

"I would think he'd have had the sense to tell you to go home," Tiffany muttered. "Now, be good! I'll be there as soon as possible."

It was difficult to walk into the hotel lobby that Monday morning. Tiffany paused just inside the big glass doors, her eyes sweeping the place. But there was no sign of Alan. Then she realized he'd probably already left for his appointment at Commonwealth Medical Center.

What had he decided to tell them?

She was thinking about this and very little else as she walked into the publicity office. Trudy was speaking to someone on the phone, and nodded in greeting. She looked pale, but especially pretty. She was wearing a soft shade of spring green that complemented her dark red hair. And her eyes, in fact, nearly matched the dress material. Tiffany could not help but smile at her. There was no denying that Trudy knew when she was needed. It would have taken a lot to keep her away today.

Seated at her own desk, Tiffany paused for a moment. There was something she had to do before she attacked the mound of mail in front of her. She lifted her phone and dialed the reception desk, and then asked if Dr. Camilla Vegas was still registered.

She was. Due to check out tomorrow morning.

The same time Alan was due to check out originally, Tiffany thought, drawing conclusions that seemed inescapable, and which she didn't like at all. But now Alan had said he was going back to Bangor tonight. Reflecting upon this, Tiffany decided that his change in plans surely indicated that he'd decided to turn down the Boston job. Which was wrong, entirely wrong.

His idea of a compromise—if his suggestion that they remarry had been that—had not been hers. Yet it certainly seemed that two adults should be capable of living in the same city without so much—so much needless trauma—involved.

From the doorway Trudy said, "Well! You're quite a picture."

Tiffany was wearing a raw silk dress printed with

violet and pink flowers. It was narrow-waisted, cinched with a tie belt of the same material and had full, bell sleeves. The snug-fitting bodice was accented by a large Victorian lace collar, and the skirt was full. It was very becoming, and she'd chosen it deliberately that morning . . . hoping she'd encounter Alan one more time in the hotel so that he'd see it on her.

She'd made up carefully, highlighting her eyes with violet shadow. And she was wearing her pearls, which went perfectly with her outfit. She'd added daubs of Royal Secret, too. If all of this seemed like a bid for Alan's attention . . . well, it was, Tiffany admitted to herself. She decided that if he didn't seek her out over the course of the day, she'd go looking for him.

She rationalized this by telling herself that she couldn't let him leave Boston without first finding out what his decision was. And if he'd made up his mind not to take the job at Commonwealth, it was up to her to try to make him change it. Otherwise, she'd no doubt at all that she was going to suffer a massive guilt complex—as she would be to blame.

"Hey," Trudy said indignantly, "I was paying you a compliment, and you look as if I slapped you instead."

"Sorry," Tiffany said. "I was about to tell you that you look lovely yourself today, even if you are an invalid and should still be home recuperating. That dress brings springtime right into the room."

"Very poetic," Trudy observed. "Look, I'm going down for coffee. Can I bring you some?"

"I'll go get it," Tiffany volunteered. "You shouldn't move around so much."

Trudy at once protested, but Tiffany was adamant. And as she crossed the lobby to the coffee shop, once again she was surreptitiously looking for Alan.

She was still looking for him when she went down to the Veranda Room for lunch with Trudy at her side. Usually they took separate lunch hours, but Tiffany had insisted that Trudy accompany her today.

"I'm going to see that you get the right kind of nourishment!" she said.

However, she merely toyed with her own shrimp salad, delicious though it was. She was nearly through with her meal when she remembered that Alan was lunching with the doctor who'd invited him to tour the Medical Center.

Your head simply isn't on straight today, she accused herself.

The afternoon seemed endless. Finally, at four o'clock, Tiffany could stand it no longer and called the front desk.

"Has Dr. Alan Winslow checked out yet?" she asked.

The answer was negative.

She had sent Trudy home at three, an act which had taken a lot of persuasion. Now she closed the door to the publicity office and walked down the corridor and past the elevator bank, heading for Alan's room.

At his door she hesitated only briefly. Then she knocked, more firmly than she'd intended.

It was a long moment before she got an answer. In the interim, she thought she heard someone talking inside the room, but decided it must be a TV in the adjoining room. Then Alan flung the door open, and she'd never seen anyone look more astonished.

"Tiffany!" he exclaimed.

He moved back, and she went on into the room. Then she stopped, frozen.

Camilla Vegas was comfortably ensconsed in an armchair, a tall drink in her hand.

"I'm sorry," Tiffany said stiffly. "I didn't mean to interrupt."

It was an unfortunate way to put it, as she gathered immediately from the annoyed expression that crossed Alan's face. But he only said, "You're not interrupting. Sit down, won't you? Could I fix you a drink? I can offer a choice of gin or bourbon."

"No, thank you," Tiffany said hastily. "I only stopped by to ask if you'd like my secretary to save any newspaper clippings we get about your meetings. We subscribe to a clipping service that covers the entire country and most of Canada."

She'd snatched at an excuse for being there, and this, at least, sounded plausible. "It's something we do for most of the groups that meet here," she added.

He said politely, "Thanks, Tiffany. That would be very much appreciated, I'm sure."

"Very well, then. I'll tell Trudy," she said, already starting to back up toward the door.

Camilla had been watching this interchange with mild amusement. "Are you sure you don't have time for a drink, Miss Richards? My husband's managed to get tomorrow off, and he's driving up from Hartford. He should be here any minute. Perhaps we could persuade Alan to delay his departure for Bangor so we could all have dinner together?"

"That would be very nice," Tiffany managed, "but I really do have to get back to my office. I let my secretary go home early," she added, feeling that Camilla deserved a bit more in the way of an explanation. "She's just recovering from emergency surgery."

"Oh?"

"She had an appendectomy only a week ago," Tiffany said. "I didn't feel that she should come back so soon but . . . well, she's a treasure. She's really devoted to the job."

"And to you, perhaps?" Camilla suggested.

"Well . . . we are very good friends."

Tiffany was at the door by the time she said this. "Nice to see you, Dr. Vegas," she managed to say to Camilla, and then turned to Alan. She couldn't meet his eyes. She couldn't. As it was, she felt herself flushing under his gaze. She was all kinds of a fool for having rushed to his room like this. At this point he must surely think that she was the most erratic individual in the world. Throughout the whole week her behavior had been anything but consistent.

"Have a good trip back to Maine," she said finally, then turned and made her way up the corridor as quickly as she could, short of actually running. She didn't pause when she came to the publicity office, but kept going on to the executive suite.

Grafton's secretary looked up and smiled a professional smile. "Did you want something, Miss Richards?" she asked.

"I'd like to see Mr. Emery if he's free," Tiffany said.

The secretary pressed the intercom button and said, "Miss Richards would like a word with you, Mr. Emery."

As she had expected he would, Grafton issued orders to send her right in.

Grafton had been reading a magazine, and he set it aside as she entered his office, favoring her with his always charming smile.

"What an unexpected pleasure," he told her.

He motioned her to a chair, and Tiffany sat down,

wondering just how to put what she wanted to say to him. Quickly she decided that the best approach would be to come right out with it.

"Grafton," she said without preamble, "I'd like to take some time off."

Grafton was an expert at camouflaging his emotions, but Tiffany had caught him off guard. His pale eyes actually bulged, and he could not have looked more astonished.

"I'm sure you have vacation time coming to you, my dear," he managed, then added, recovering quickly, "But I thought we'd agreed that you'd stay at your post until we find the right assistant for you."

"I know," Tiffany agreed. "But we haven't exactly been pursuing the search."

This was true enough. It was a matter to which she usually didn't give much thought, because she didn't especially want an assistant. Working with Mike Haggerty had been wonderful, but she couldn't imagine sharing her job with anyone else. And even though she would now be the department head, of course, it still would be sharing.

Grafton, sounding faintly aggrieved, said, "I suppose we have been lax, Tiffany. But you've been doing so well by yourself that I haven't pressed the point. Also, I've had the idea that you prefer to work alone."

There were times when Grafton was too astute, especially when it served his own interests. He had a knack for putting a person on the defensive when it was in his own interest, too. Tiffany became determined that this was not going to happen to her.

"It's true that I haven't pressed the point, Grafton," she conceded, "and that's probably because I've had Trudy Barnes as my secretary."

"She's that efficient?"

"She's more than efficient," Tiffany told him. "She has a real feeling for her job and an astonishing amount of information right at her fingertips. Sally Grant was an excellent temporary replacement. She was wonderful, in fact. But there's no one else quite like Trudy, as I found out last week."

"Then," Grafton suggested, "perhaps you should groom her to become assistant. It wouldn't be the first time we've promoted from within the ranks. When that's possible, as a matter of fact, it's always an excellent morale booster."

Tiffany shook her head. "Trudy doesn't want to be my assistant," she said bluntly. "I thought of the possibility some time ago and spoke to her about it. She refused, point blank. She likes what she's doing; she has no desire to move to the executive level. And that's what it would be, of course. If I were to leave, she'd be in line to become publicity director."

"If you were to leave," Grafton echoed. "What is this, Tiffany? Is there something you're not telling me?"

"No."

"I don't detect a honeymoon in the offing, do I?" Grafton asked, blatantly fishing.

"No, you do not," Tiffany said levelly.

"You can't blame me for wondering, my dear. I saw that little scene with your ex-husband out on the sidewalk the other day. Also, the whole town knows how Hank Carella feels about you. Two candidates for your hand, eh, Tiffany?"

"That doesn't even deserve an answer," she snapped, and Grafton looked properly hurt.

"Very well," he said. "To go back to your request,

though, I think what we shall have to do is to become more energetic in our search for an assistant for you. But until we're successful in that search, I don't see how I can authorize time off for you. If it were an emergency—an illness, such as Trudy just had—there would be no alternative, of course. But I can't endorse your going off on a holiday and leaving the office without anyone to head it."

There was a moment of brief, intense silence. Then Tiffany said coolly, "What makes you think I want to go off on a holiday, Grafton?"

"It's a logical conclusion, wouldn't you say?" he countered.

"Not necessarily. I think the bottom line here is that I'm entitled to time off . . . and what I do with it is my own concern."

She'd not intended to speak so sharply, yet once she'd said this, she had no regrets about it. Grafton deserved to hear the truth occasionally.

She rose. "I'm sorry, Grafton," she said. "I wouldn't think of leaving Trudy this week. She's come back much sooner than she should have. As a matter of fact, I thought you'd tell her so when you saw her in the office this morning and even suggest that she go home."

"Tiffany . . ." he began, but she cut him off.

"As I've said," she continued, "I wouldn't think of leaving Trudy alone this week. But I shall not be coming in on Saturday, and you may expect me to be absent for a week after that, maybe longer." She drew a deep breath. "If you wish to consider it absence without leave and fire me, then I shall have to accept that," she concluded.

* * *

It was the first time Tiffany had ever issued an ultimatum, and she felt a bit heady about it as she went back to her own office. She would have given a great deal to have been able to take a picture of Grafton's face when she'd told him he could fire her. He'd looked absolutely thunderstruck.

He'd treated her thereafter as if she were a troubled child. He'd been soothing, cajoling, walking her to the door and reminding her to think this over and to get back to him in a couple of days when, he was sure, things would look "different" to her.

Tiffany was already sure, though, that things were not going to look different at all. Not, at least, in the sense Grafton was talking about. Come the weekend, she didn't know what she was going to do. But she did know that she was going to leave Boston. Maybe she'd fly to Bermuda, maybe she'd jet to Paris or London for a week, maybe she'd just go out to Nantucket and enjoy the quaint charm of that famous old island off the Massachusetts coast.

The word *island* struck at her. No, wherever she might go it wouldn't be Nantucket, or any other island, Islands would always remind her of Maine, of Alan.

She wondered if he'd left Boston yet and was already on his way back to Bangor. She found herself hoping fervently that he hadn't. Although she'd said good-bye to him, there at the door of his room, there was the chance that he might still try to get in touch with her, and right now she was more than willing to agree to anything he might suggest. Cocktails. Dinner. A moonlight stroll along the Esplanade.

She was even ready to talk about the past, if that's what he wanted. Though, she told herself almost shyly, the time had come when she'd much rather talk about the future.

But there was no message. And when, an hour later, Tiffany called down to the registration desk, unable to bear the suspense any longer, she was told that Dr. Alan Winslow had already checked out.

Chapter Fifteen

The hotel was especially busy that week. There was a major convention in the house, several small group meetings and both a stamp and an antique show. Tiffany had little time in which to think about anything.

Hank Carella was a frequent visitor during this period, dropping in at the publicity office several times a day. But it was not until the week was almost over that Tiffany began to guess the reason for this.

Trudy. She'd lost weight as a result of her recent surgery, and she was still rather pale. But the combination had yielded very interesting results. There was a new, almost wistful quality about her that was very appealing.

Trudy seemed completely unaware of Hank's interest. Everyone on the hotel staff had gossiped about Hank Carella's interest in Tiffany, and Trudy obviously thought this was the reason for his frequent appearances now. So thinking that Hank was only concerned with her employer, Trudy was herself when he came in to visit. And Hank was becoming more captivated every day. Tiffany had no doubt of it and was delighted.

Hank came by Friday afternoon just as Tiffany and Trudy were about to shut up the office. Grafton had capitulated to Tiffany's request for time off out of necessity. Tiffany had made it clear that she was not going to change her mind about this, and both girls were preparing to celebrate her upcoming "vacation." Now Hank suggested that they let him join them.

They opted to go somewhere outside the hotel, and so Hank led them to a small, intimate bar that suited their moods perfectly. The women ordered frosty strawberry daiquiris while he, grimacing at their taste, chose Irish whiskey on the rocks.

They were well into their drinks when Hank turned to Tiffany to say, "What's this about your going off on a rest cure?"

She laughed. "Well, I wouldn't exactly put it that way."

"Grafton told me that it was more or less mandatory. He gave the impression it might even be an enforced rest, on doctor's orders."

Was Hank emphasizing the word *doctor?*

Tiffany looked at him suspiciously. But she only said, "That's all in Grafton's imagination. I just want to get away for a few days."

"Going someplace special?"

"No," she said, and added honestly, "I haven't even decided where I'm going yet. Out of the city, that's all."

To her relief, Hank changed the subject. But a few minutes later he said, as casually as if he weren't exploding a bomb, "Too bad about Alan Winslow and Commonwealth Medical Center."

Tiffany tensed, but before she could speak, Trudy asked, "What about Dr. Winslow and Commonwealth, Hank?"

"Well, he'd been invited to join the staff," Hank said.

"Yes. You told me that, Tiffany," Trudy pointed out.

Tiffany put down her daiquiri because her hand was shaking. "What about Alan and the staff job, Hank?" she asked him.

"We're doing a segment on the new medical center for the show," Hank said, as if he were talking about something that was not at all earthshaking. "I had a talk with Dr. Anthony Donato the other day, who heads the surgical staff . . ."

"I know that," Tiffany interrupted impatiently.

"Well, he mentioned that he'd caught my show the night I had Alan Winslow and those other doctors on it. He told me how impressed he is with Winslow, and how he wished he'd joined the staff at Commonwealth. That is going to be quite a facility."

Hank continued talking about the hospital and the place it would play on the Boston medical scene, but Tiffany didn't hear a word of what he was saying. She was more than willing to let Trudy be Hank's rapt, attentive audience right now. Her own worst fears had been confirmed. Alan had turned down the job.

She'd hoped against hope that she'd been wrong in assuming this was what he'd done. She'd hoped that he had accepted the staff position and was winding up his affairs in Maine. Then he'd be moving to Boston. And—as he'd said in so many words—it wasn't that large a place. One day they'd be certain to run into each other. And when they did, she wasn't going to let history repeat itself. She was going to . . .

"Tiffany?" Hank's voice broke into her reverie.

"Yes?" she responded absently.

"Can I interest you in another drink?"

"No, thanks," she said, and got up before either Hank or Trudy realized what she was about to do. "Look, I've got to run along, but you two stay and have another one," she suggested. "And, Trudy . . ."

"Yes?" Trudy said, looking at Hank uncertainly as if she expected him to veto Tiffany's suggestion.

"Don't take the whole weight of the world on your shoulders while I'm away," Tiffany advised. "Rob will help you, and if you need some really super advice," she finished, grinning at both of them mischievously, "don't hesitate to call on Hank!"

Tiffany stayed home Saturday. She spent the day cleaning house, putting away some of her winter clothes and weeding out her spring-summer wardrobe. She kept herself very busy, but it was impossible to forget what Hank had said about Alan.

She felt very much to blame for his decision. And, as she sprayed some of her wool sweaters with mothproofing before storing them away, she berated herself for being all kinds of a fool.

Long, long ago, she should have had the courage to face Alan and talk things out with him. But she had been too . . . too selfish, she decided, wincing away from this word and yet knowing it was the right one. She'd been so beset by her own grief over Chad that she'd never really considered Alan's feelings at all; she'd been so sure that he was totally absorbed by his work.

Remembering this, she wondered that he'd wanted to have anything to do with her when they'd met again in the hotel. She marveled that he'd thought up the idea of going out to lunch and pretending it was a first date. And the fact that he would suggest that she 'come back,' that they remarry, seemed completely incredible.

Could he possibly love her that much?

This was the question that haunted Tiffany throughout the day, the night, and all of Sunday as well. As usual, she'd gone across to the bakery on Sunday morning and had come home with golden brown brioche. As she buttered them and ate them with delicious apricot jam, all she could think about was that she wished Alan were here to share them with her.

Maybe he *had* loved her that much. This was the conclusion she'd reached after hours of thinking about it. But if so, something had happened . . . and it had happened on the island in Maine. Something had caused Alan to have a change of heart.

She couldn't blame him. Even though she ached at the thought of it, she couldn't blame him. But no matter how much his feelings for her might have changed, she owed him something. She owed him the right to come to Boston and to feel free about it . . . if it wasn't too late.

That Sunday Tiffany even went so far as to look up Dr. Anthony Donato's number in the telephone directory, but he wasn't listed. Then she wondered what she would have said to him if he had been.

"This is Tiffany Winslow, doctor. I want you to give my ex-husband another chance, because it's my fault he turned down your offer to be on the staff at Commonwealth."

She could imagine how that would go over with a physician of Dr. Donato's caliber . . . and how Alan would react when he learned that she'd meddled in his professional affairs. By Monday morning Tiffany, after a sleepless night, had come to a decision.

Like a general planning a campaign, she mapped her strategy. Then she packed carefully, and this done, she called the garage and asked them to send the car around.

Spring was, again, proving to be capricious. It was drizzling as Tiffany drove out of Boston, and it was raining hard by the time she neared the traffic circle at Portsmouth, New Hampshire.

Every mile she'd traveled had reminded her of Alan. And by the time she'd crossed the bridge and was heading into Maine she was beginning to feel very unsure of herself.

She should have called him first. But there was no way of knowing what he would have said. She remembered only too well her own elusiveness in the past when he'd tried to contact her or, much more recently, when he'd tried to get her into any sort of deep conversation. He could play the same sort of game. Except that . . . it hadn't been a game with her when she was doing it, nor would it be with him now.

The truth could simply be that he really didn't want to see her anymore. He'd made his own decisions, and he was going his own way. If this were not the case, she thought miserably as she peered ahead while the windshield wiper clicked furiously, he would certainly have gotten in touch with her during the week.

The rain got heavier and heavier as she neared Portland. She was tempted to turn off and find a place where she could get some coffee. But there was no indication that the rain was about to abate; it wasn't something you could wait out. Not, at least, when you were as impatient to reach your destination as she was.

Still, driving in weather like this took a heavy toll on the nerves. And Tiffany hadn't fully realized how far it was to Bangor. Once she was past Brunswick, past the place where Alan had turned onto Route 1, she was traveling in entirely unfamiliar territory. And it seemed to her that she'd been going forever before eventually she saw a sign that said, "Bangor, 20 miles."

Her first impression of Bangor was a watery one. Despite the valiant efforts of the windshield wiper, water was streaming down the glass. Ahead, Tiffany saw a motel sign and turned in, praying that there'd be a room for her. There was, a very pleasant room, and she'd never felt so grateful for living space before.

She went into the bathroom and ran a hot tub. There was a trial-size package of bubble bath in her cosmetic case, and she splurged and used the whole thing. Then she luxuriated in the hot bath for a long, long time. She'd been chilled to the bone on arrival. Not that it was cold; it was the dampness that got to her. Now, finally, she felt warm all through.

Her next step was a consultation with the phone directory. Alan Winslow, M.D., was listed, she saw to her relief. She'd never been in Bangor before, so street addresses meant nothing to her. But she assumed this must be his home.

She glanced at her watch. It was just after two. Probably there wasn't much chance that Alan would be home at this hour. On the other hand, this might be a day off for him. It was worth taking the chance.

She placed the call, and the phone was answered on the third ring. But it was not Alan's voice Tiffany heard, but that of a woman with a distinct Down East accent.

Fortunately, she didn't ask for Tiffany's name, because Tiffany didn't want to give it. She didn't want to identify herself as Miss Richards, and certainly she was not about to call herself Mrs. Winslow. She was relieved when the woman, evidently Alan's housekeeper, assumed that she was a patient.

"The doctor's at the hospital, miss," she said. "I don't expect him back for a while. You could try him there if you like," she added, and gave Tiffany the number.

In the past Tiffany had seldom called Alan at the hospital. It had been almost impossible to reach him most of the time, and on occasions when she'd left a message and he had eventually called back, he'd sounded so harried.

Out of habit she hesitated. But then she placed the second call, and heard the responding, "Eastern Maine Medical Center" at the end of the wire.

Again, though, it wasn't easy to reach Dr. Winslow. The operator, checking, revealed that he was still in surgery, and suggested that Tiffany try again in an hour or so.

But Tiffany knew she couldn't wait that long.

It was still pouring out, but that didn't matter. Much as she wanted to dress up for this occasion to look her very best, Tiffany settled for a gray pant suit that had been a basic part of her wardrobe for a long time. With it, she wore a bright yellow sweater. Then she slung her trusty poncho around her shoulders and started out again.

The desk clerk gave her directions to Eastern Maine

Medical Center, and fortunately it wasn't difficult to find. The hospital complex bordered the Penobscot River at the far end of the town. It was an impressive facility. Some of the original buildings were still in use, but a big, very modern wing had been added, and it dominated the whole scene.

Tiffany found a parking space as near to the entrance as possible, then dashed through the heavy rain. Inside the hospital lobby a receptionist obligingly placed a call to Dr. Alan Winslow for her, but there was no immediate answer. Evidently he was still in surgery, Tiffany decided, and she settled down in a comfortable armchair to wait until he was free.

Resolutely, she told herself that she'd wait all night, if necessary.

As it happened, Alan was just coming out of surgery when Tiffany called, and then had to make delayed afternoon rounds. The staff knew that he didn't like to be disturbed when he was visiting his patients unless there was a real emergency, and for this reason Tiffany's message was not immediately relayed to him.

Rounds finished, he went into the doctor's lounge and poured himself a cup of coffee. He paused for a moment at the window, looking out at the driving rain. It was a dismal day, and—despite the fact that he'd just performed a very delicate operation that almost certainly was going to be a success—the weather matched his mood.

All week he'd had second thoughts about coming back to Bangor so abruptly. But it had seemed the best thing to do at the time. He'd felt strongly that he and Tiffany needed some space between them. When they were together, it was much too easy for both of them to capitulate physically . . . and wonderful though that was, he wanted more from her.

She had not reacted at all to his suggestion of a compromise. In fact, she'd looked totally stunned when he'd asked her to come back to him, to marry him again. To him, the expression on her face had indicated rejection as surely as anything could.

Dozing in the armchair while keeping the fire burning, he'd come to a few conclusions. One was that he'd been a fool to try to rush Tiffany as he had; certainly he'd been an idiot to embark with her on that wild escapade out to the island. He'd played the macho role to the hilt, he'd acted as if cavemen were back in style again. He couldn't blame her if he'd completely turned her off.

He'd been staggered when she'd come to his hotel room the next afternoon. And he would have given a great deal to have been there alone at the time. Camilla's presence had been inhibiting, to say the least. And Camilla had teased the hell out of him for what she called his "schoolboy" behavior toward Tiffany.

Still, in retrospect, it seemed to him that it had been a mistake simply to walk out of Boston as he had. But then, this had been an extremely busy week; he'd gone home exhausted each night. His head had not been clear enough to think up a new plan of action. And he wasn't about to rush off and start tilting at windmills again. The next approach, he told himself, was going to have to be considerably more rational.

He picked up a copy of the *New England Journal of Medicine* and settled down, skimming through the magazine as he drank his coffee. His beeper sounded, and reluctantly—he'd had enough on his surgical plate for one day—he turned it off and went over to the phone. There was a young lady waiting for him in the downstairs lobby. She said her name was Tiffany.

From where Tiffany was sitting in the lobby there was a clear view of a long corridor leading into the inner regions of the hospital. She'd been trying to focus on a well-thumbed fashion magazine she'd found in a nearby rack when she looked up and saw Alan.

He was still wearing his surgical greens, and it was with a shock that she realized this was the first time she'd ever seen him in them. They made him look taller, more slender, but there was still that width to his shoulders and a latent sense of power about him. He always walked with a confidence she envied.

Seeing him dressed in the working garb of his profession set him apart to Tiffany. He seemed magnified to her, and she felt more than a little in awe of him. But as he came closer, she saw that he looked very tired, older. There were deep shadows beneath his eyes and lines of strain around his mouth. And he looked pale. Surprisingly pale.

Suddenly he saw her. For an instant he stopped, as if he couldn't believe his own eyes. She couldn't have described the expression that crossed his face; she only knew that she felt as if everything inside her was being twisted, and she nearly cried out from the pain of it. Then she was on her feet, running, actually running, out of the lobby and down the corridor to meet him. And the entire world could have been watching for all she cared as she flung herself into his arms.

At once she rallied. She pulled away just as quickly, appalled because she was making a spectacle of herself, and undoubtedly embarrassing him very much. He had stature here in this hospital; he was an eminent surgeon; he . . .

She caught the unexpected glint of laughter in his eyes, and he said, "Would you mind repeating that, please?"

"What?" she asked, confused.

"Would you mind acting out your first reaction again?" he asked politely. And then he helped her, drawing her into the circle of his arms while his mouth found hers, his kiss answering so many questions. So many questions.

Like Tiffany, Alan wouldn't have cared if the entire population of the universe had been on hand to watch them. As far as he was concerned, he and Tiffany were alone.

By mutual consent they went back to Tiffany's motel.

"Mrs. Malone is a terrific housekeeper," Alan had said with a laugh, "but she'd want to fuss over you, and she'd insist on fixing supper for both of us. Another time, eh?"

"Another time," she'd agreed happily.

He'd changed into dark brown slacks and an old tweed jacket. He looked comfortable and relaxed, and Tiffany was sure that he must be the handsomest man in the world.

It was all she could do to keep her hands off him.

The room had been divided, so that it was part living room, part bedroom. Alan was sitting on the couch, his legs spread out in front of him. He said, "I went back to the island this past weekend."

"Oh?" she asked.

"I'm thinking of selling it," he told her. This was true. If Tiffany wasn't going to be a part of his life he didn't want the island, he didn't want anything.

Tiffany was appalled. "You can't do that," she blurted.

"Why not?" he asked mildly. Then added, "I'd no longer enjoy it by myself."

"But it's your . . . your own oasis," she protested. "And . . . there's no need for you to sell it anyway. I mean . . ."

His tone was gentle. "Just what do you mean, Tiffany?"

"You asked me a question the other night," she reminded him. "But you never gave me a chance to answer it."

"Come on!" he protested.

"It's true. Before I could get over the shock of what you'd asked and say anything you . . . you started to make love to me."

"And?"

"I don't have much resistance when you start making love to me," Tiffany said, avoiding his eyes. "I stop being very coherent. So . . ."

"Yes?"

"So you didn't give me the chance to say yes," she said, the last words spoken in almost a whisper.

Alan stared at her so blankly that her heart lurched. Now it was she who felt rejection; she wished she could literally crawl into the wall or disappear out through the window into the thickly falling rain.

Then he said, "Tiff . . . please."

His voice was husky, and she saw that his eyes had turned dark charcoal again. He said, "Unless you really mean what I think you mean . . . please, for God's sake . . ."

Unsteadily she said, "I should have added: if you'll have me."

"Have you?" He groaned. "Oh, my God!" he whispered abjectly, and leaned forward, holding his head in his hands.

"Alan," she prodded, but he didn't answer her. "Alan," she tried again, "remember what you said about mirror images? You see yourself one way but actually . . . well, you're just the reverse? I've been looking at myself in the mirror, and I haven't liked what I've seen. Because I know now that I never gave you a chance."

He looked up, his face haggard. He said, "The night Chad died there was a terrible auto accident. Five teenagers were brought into the emergency room. We were short staffed . . . and I, at least, wasn't all that experienced. At first we didn't think any of them had a chance. But we worked on them all night; we saved three of them. . . ." His voice trailed off. Then he finished, huskily, "I'm not trying to excuse myself."

"Oh, my dearest," Tiffany said, the words wrung out of her. "You have nothing to excuse yourself for. I was so blind!"

They met each other halfway, and they clung together. Tears came, passion temporarily receding as a different sort of love suffused them.

After a long time Alan said shakily, "I can't believe you're really here."

"It took all my courage to come to you," Tiffany confessed, her own voice trembling. "But when I heard you'd refused Dr. Donato's offer, I had to do something. It would have been so wrong for you not to go to Boston."

He stared down at her. "I didn't refuse Donato's offer," he told her, puzzled. "I have another six weeks here to finish things up. Then I'm going to Commonwealth. I realized last Monday that the only way I'd ever have a chance of getting you back was to move into your territory. At least," he amended, and now his gray eyes were as clear as the rain falling outside, "that's what I thought."

She was about to tell him that Hank had told her otherwise about his decision, but then she paused. Actually, Hank had told her very little except to raise the subject of Alan and Dr. Donato. From this, she'd drawn her own conclusions. And, she added, smiling to herself, she'd be forever grateful to Hank for having led her astray.

"We have so much to talk about, darling," Alan said softly. "So much to catch up on."

Tiffany smiled up at him. "We've the rest of our lives in which to talk," she told him.

"True." He nodded. And as he reached out eager arms to draw her to him, to claim her, she knew he was no more in the mood to talk than she was. In fact, she doubted if they'd be doing much talking at all for quite some time to come.

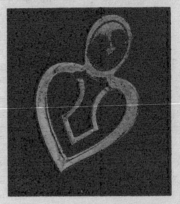

MORE ROMANCE FOR
A SPECIAL WAY TO RELAX
$1.95 each

2 ☐ Hastings	21 ☐ Hastings	41 ☐ Halston	60 ☐ Thorne
3 ☐ Dixon	22 ☐ Howard	42 ☐ Drummond	61 ☐ Beckman
4 ☐ Vitek	23 ☐ Charles	43 ☐ Shaw	62 ☐ Bright
5 ☐ Converse	24 ☐ Dixon	44 ☐ Eden	63 ☐ Wallace
6 ☐ Douglass	25 ☐ Hardy	45 ☐ Charles	64 ☐ Converse
7 ☐ Stanford	26 ☐ Scott	46 ☐ Howard	65 ☐ Cates
8 ☐ Halston	27 ☐ Wisdom	47 ☐ Stephens	66 ☐ Mikels
9 ☐ Baxter	28 ☐ Ripy	48 ☐ Ferrell	67 ☐ Shaw
10 ☐ Thiels	29 ☐ Bergen	49 ☐ Hastings	68 ☐ Sinclair
11 ☐ Thornton	30 ☐ Stephens	50 ☐ Browning	69 ☐ Dalton
12 ☐ Sinclair	31 ☐ Baxter	51 ☐ Trent	70 ☐ Clare
13 ☐ Beckman	32 ☐ Douglass	52 ☐ Sinclair	71 ☐ Skillern
14 ☐ Keene	33 ☐ Palmer	53 ☐ Thomas	72 ☐ Belmont
15 ☐ James	35 ☐ James	54 ☐ Hohl	73 ☐ Taylor
16 ☐ Carr	36 ☐ Dailey	55 ☐ Stanford	74 ☐ Wisdom
17 ☐ John	37 ☐ Stanford	56 ☐ Wallace	75 ☐ John
18 ☐ Hamilton	38 ☐ John	57 ☐ Thornton	76 ☐ Ripy
19 ☐ Shaw	39 ☐ Milan	58 ☐ Douglass	77 ☐ Bergen
20 ☐ Musgrave	40 ☐ Converse	59 ☐ Roberts	78 ☐ Gladstone

$2.25 each

79 ☐ Hastings	82 ☐ McKenna	85 ☐ Beckman	88 ☐ Saxon
80 ☐ Douglass	83 ☐ Major	86 ☐ Halston	89 ☐ Meriwether
81 ☐ Thornton	84 ☐ Stephens	87 ☐ Dixon	90 ☐ Justin

Silhouette Special Edition

$2.25 each

91 ☐ Stanford	109 ☐ Beckman	127 ☐ Taylor	145 ☐ Wallace
92 ☐ Hamilton	110 ☐ Browning	128 ☐ Macomber	146 ☐ Thornton
93 ☐ Lacey	111 ☐ Thorne	129 ☐ Rowe	147 ☐ Dalton
94 ☐ Barrie	112 ☐ Belmont	130 ☐ Carr	148 ☐ Gordon
95 ☐ Doyle	113 ☐ Camp	131 ☐ Lee	149 ☐ Claire
96 ☐ Baxter	114 ☐ Ripy	132 ☐ Dailey	150 ☐ Dailey
97 ☐ Shaw	115 ☐ Halston	133 ☐ Douglass	151 ☐ Shaw
98 ☐ Hurley	116 ☐ Roberts	134 ☐ Ripy	152 ☐ Adams
99 ☐ Dixon	117 ☐ Converse	135 ☐ Seger	153 ☐ Sinclair
100 ☐ Roberts	118 ☐ Jackson	136 ☐ Scott	154 ☐ Malek
101 ☐ Bergen	119 ☐ Langan	137 ☐ Parker	155 ☐ Lacey
102 ☐ Wallace	120 ☐ Dixon	138 ☐ Thornton	156 ☐ Hastings
103 ☐ Taylor	121 ☐ Shaw	139 ☐ Halston	157 ☐ Taylor
104 ☐ Wallace	122 ☐ Walker	140 ☐ Sinclair	158 ☐ Charles
105 ☐ Sinclair	123 ☐ Douglass	141 ☐ Saxon	159 ☐ Camp
106 ☐ John	124 ☐ Mikels	142 ☐ Bergen	160 ☐ Wisdom
107 ☐ Ross	125 ☐ Cates	143 ☐ Bright	161 ☐ Stanford
108 ☐ Stephens	126 ☐ Wildman	144 ☐ Meriwether	162 ☐ Roberts

SILHOUETTE SPECIAL EDITION, Department SE/2
1230 Avenue of the Americas
New York, NY 10020

Please send me the books I have checked above. I am enclosing $_____ (please add 75¢ to cover postage and handling. NYS and NYC residents please add appropriate sales tax). Send check or money order—no cash or C.O.D.'s please. Allow six weeks for delivery.

NAME _____

ADDRESS _____

CITY _____ STATE/ZIP _____

Coming Next Month

Something Lost, Something Gained by Carole Halston

Megan had been nervous about her big fashion writing assignment in the Caribbean, but when she found out her photographer partner was Case Ballantine, her ex-husband, she knew her toughest challenge would be to win him back to her side.

Firebird by Margaret Ripy

Three years before, Lindsey had refused to give up her career as a prima ballerina to follow Brazilian tycoon Jared St. Martin to the Amazon. Now Jared was back—and this time Lindsey knew she'd find it impossible to resist his fire.

· End Of Illusion by Amanda Lee

Kate had a ten-year-old son who needed a man's influence. Morgan Chandler had a teen-aged daughter in need of a woman's hand. Morgan's proposal that they become a family was tempting, but did he long for her as a woman as well as a wife?

Dream Of Yesterday by Nancy John

Kirstie had been too young when she first loved Adam Prescott. When they finally met again, another woman came to claim him. But Adam still wanted Kirstie more than any woman— and he was determined to have her.

Hearts In Exile by Ann Hurley

Cally and Jesse had shared many a madcap adventure while growing up on the Texas coast. Years later, they met again on a faraway shore. But how could their love last when one heart was in exile, too proud to look homeward?

Male Order Bride by Carolyn Thornton

Rafe Chancellor had beseiged Lacey Adams with a barrage of whimsical messages and gifts just to convince her to date him. He soon won Lacey's heart, but was this charming man also game for an old-fashioned commitment?